Earth LEGEND

by

Florence Witkop

Published Take Me Away Books, a division of Winged Publications

Copyright © 2017 by Florence Witkop

ISBN-13: 978-1-946939-34-0
ISBN-10: 1-946939-34-X

Chapter One

I shouldn't have been there. But …

"We need someone to bring the Range Rover home for my sister." Betts looked at me through tearful eyes. "Because we're not coming back." She held out a slip of cardboard. "We have an extra ID."

My shoulders sagged. "Okay." Betts and Todd and Shawn and Janet were ready to go, two couples in shorts and tee shirts. They looked like normal, average, nice people going on an outing. They weren't, of course, but if anyone was perfect for this job, it was my cousins. "I'll drive you there and bring the Range Rover back."

Todd threw his arms around me. "Thanks, cousin." His voice was hoarse. He was pretending to be tough but that voice said it all. He was scared. Terrified. But determined.

As were they all. Their chances of success were next to zero and if I was with them when they got caught, I could be thrown in jail too. But what they were planning was important, never mind that it was illegal. They'd tried legal channels and been shut out at every turn. There was no time left so there was nothing to do except become felons.

We climbed into the Range Rover and I took it onto the freeway. The trip went smoothly until we neared the space complex, namely the building that housed the bottom of the elevator that took people and freight to the space station. The building was huge, having grown as the space program grew until now it was as large as several football fields. But it wasn't big enough to hold the entire complement of the Destiny and everyone who wanted to say goodbye to them at once so the colonists had to say their goodbyes in increments. Today's group was the last, which meant it was my cousins last chance to mingle with them and become stowaways.

Near the complex, congestion was bad and quickly got worse. I had to slow to a crawl as people ran onto the freeway waving signs and yelling. Wannabe colonists who were passed over because their genes carried the potential for diseases that shouldn't be exported to the larger universe. People who believed their genes were superior enough that they should have been selected over those who were chosen to colonize the galaxy. Both groups were furious that they'd been ignored and were out in force and screaming epithets. All were angry enough to destroy the Destiny and everyone aboard rather than be left behind themselves.

As we left the freeway and drew closer to the complex, the crowd turned ugly. I couldn't shut out the chanting any more than I could block the rotten vegetables smashing against our windows as I threaded the Range Rover through hoards of people spilling over the road and anywhere else they could fit.

A tomato splashed across the windshield, forcing me to turn on the wipers. I stopped until it cleared, and then moved again, but slower as Shawn said quietly from the back seat, "We have to do this, you know. We have to."

A face pasted itself to the window, trying to get in. To get us. Betts turned away and concentrated on the five of us in the car, chanting the mantra that had got them this far. "We must get through. We must be on the Destiny. If we aren't, they'll die. They'll all die."

Shawn's face was drawn. "Don't worry, we'll make it. We'll stow away and when things get bad, we'll be there, and we'll know what to do." Because we knew things no one else knew. Because we could do things no one else could do.

We reached the complex. Men and women who'd chained themselves to the fence were dragged in the mud as the gates opened and guards checked our fake IDs. We all held our breaths until we passed inspection and were waved into the parking garage. Todd flexed his shoulders and took a gulp of air. "We made it this far." He took in all of us in a sweeping look. "We'll do it. We'll succeed."

When we climbed from the car, we stood unmoving for a moment and savored the comparative quiet. We could still hear the calls, the chants, the concentrated howl from outside but it was lower. Quieter. We could ignore it.

Todd squared his shoulders and led the way towards the doors beyond which the colonists and crew of the Destiny were saying goodbye to their loved ones. Whole families were going whenever possible so there weren't many relatives being left behind, but there were tons of friends and hordes of media types. He turned to us grimly. "It's time."

We pushed open the doors in silence and stepped inside. If we didn't know better, we'd have thought we were watching any group of people saying goodbye to loved ones before leaving on a journey, and so we were, except that this journey would take ten thousand people far beyond the solar system. So this goodbye was permanent. Forever.

This was the last group, the last five hundred. The rest had said their goodbyes and were already on board the Destiny so now was our last chance to sneak some of us on board. If we were to save their lives, failure wasn't an option.

We looked over the room. People were already being separated into two groups at the urging of the security guards. Colonists were being shooed to the far side of the barricade a crew was erecting. Those staying behind were on the side nearest to us.

"It took too long to get through the protesters. They are ready to leave."

"We have to try."

"The guards aren't looking."

Todd and Betts sauntered casually but deliberately towards the colonists, looking in every respect as if they belonged. Two people among five hundred. Surely they'd not be noticed.

"Sir." A guard tapped Todd on the shoulder, and

then Betts. "You too, Miss. Time to leave." He steered them politely back across the barricade, patting a lethal looking gun strapped to his side in a seemingly random gesture, but no one was fooled. He knew they didn't belong. He'd use that gun if necessary. No terrorists would get on board if he had anything to say about it.

Todd and Betts retreated, Betts biting her lower lip to hold back tears and surreptitiously looking towards Shawn and Janet. She and Todd had been caught but maybe Shawn and Janet would make it.

They didn't. Another guard, a pair of them actually, was already pushing Shawn and Janet away from the colonists. They didn't even try to be gentle and their guns were drawn. The crowd beyond the complex must have the guards spooked. They weren't taking any chances on letting someone on board who could blow everyone up. Shawn and Janet were roughly thrust back towards our little group.

They'd failed. We'd all failed, in a way, because, though I wasn't going, they were my cousins and I'd been involved in the planning, along with a couple dozen other relatives. But it had all been for nothing.

Soon the colonists would be herded through doors to waiting elevators, and then whooshed up to the space station. The families and friends they'd left behind would go home and watch the launch of the Destiny on TV and think about the future their relatives would have. Envy them, perhaps.

The thing was, those colonists who were going so bravely into space wouldn't make it to the new world the astronomers were sure would support life. Some time in the future, when earth received messages from the Destiny that they were dying and nothing could be done to save them, we cousins could tell each other that it wasn't our fault, that we'd tried ... and we'd be right. We'd done our best. We had the degrees, the knowledge and the experience going back thousands of years that could keep the colonists alive in deep space.

Yes, we could say that we'd tried and failed, and it was true that nothing we tried had worked. We'd applied to be part of the crew and been rejected. We'd signed up as colonists and been rejected for that, too. Not the right genetic makeup, we'd been told. There was something slightly odd about our genes and they could only allow healthy people onto a multi-generational ship with a good but small medical facility. The very thing that made us essential also made us rejects.

My cousins refused to give up. When the rest of the family said there was nothing more to be done Todd and Betts and Shawn and Janet said they could do it. They could slip among the colonists and stow away. They were dressed right, they looked like colonists. They were perfect in every respect. They should have succeeded. But they didn't.

The agony of such a profoundly awful failure was reflected in our eyes as we stared at each other in the middle of that crowd. We couldn't hide our thoughts from each other and soon all five of us were searching for somewhere private in which to melt down. Some place away from the doomed people on the other side of the barricade

"Miss." I turned at the tap on my shoulder. An elderly guard stood a discreet couple of feet away. He pointed across the room to the colonists and crew of the Destiny. The group my cousins had failed to join. "It's getting late, Miss." The guard put a friendly hand on my shoulder and turned me towards the colonists. Then he gave me a slight shove, trying to hurry me along without being obviously pushy. "It's time to leave. You'd best finish saying goodbye to your friends and return to your family."

It took a moment for the five of us to figure out what he was talking about. Then we saw the family he was pointing towards and we took a collective breath and held it. Because among the doomed colonists was a family with the same red hair I'd been plagued with since birth. Two red-headed parents and four girls slightly younger than me but all with the same long, insanely curly carrot red hair that I'd been teased about ever since I could remember. We could easily be sisters. The guard thought we were sisters.

Miracle of miracles, when we'd dressed that morning, both that family and I, we'd all chosen tan shorts and purple tee shirts. The guard, with his black hair, couldn't know that red-heads sometimes wear purple just to shout to the world that, contrary to popular belief, red-heads can wear anything they wish. Because of my clothes and coloring, he thought I was a member of that family. He thought I was a colonist. He was shooing me towards the very group of people my cousins had failed to infiltrate.

I looked away from the red-headed family and towards my cousins as it hit us all at the same moment. Failure could be turned into success. All that was necessary was for me to take their places on the Destiny. To stow away in their stead. To carry out their mission. To become a felon. We shared the same upbringing, the same background, the same genes, and I certainly had the formal education to validate my inborn knowledge. A brand-new doctorate and several lesser degrees. I was a young but knowledgeable botanist. I could do it. I could save ten thousand lives.

My cousins' lightning-fast looks hit me with the force of bricks, the kind that usually fly through windows with messages wrapped around them. Their looks were that hard and said, 'We failed, Elle, but you can succeed.' 'We weren't able to stow away on the Destiny, and here you are being escorted on board.' 'You must do this, Elle.' 'It's your destiny.'

So I hugged each of them as they whispered advice and sobbed because they knew I'd missed the intensive sessions on how to stow away successfully. I'd have to wing it once I was on board.

As the guard pulled at my shoulder, Betts hugged me one more time and shoved something into my pocket. Then I followed that guard across the empty space that now separated the colonists from everyone else and through the small opening left where the divider hadn't yet been erected. As I passed, someone closed it behind me. I was the last colonist.

I walked straight and as tall as my five-foot-two

allowed, pretending I belonged and ignoring the curious looks aimed at me, the last person to be shooed towards a future on another planet. I didn't turn as I reached the elevators that the first few colonists were entering. Didn't look around for fear of being recognized for what I was. A stowaway.

As I passed through the door, though, I couldn't help it. I did turn just enough to wave to my cousins because I'd never see them again and I was terrified. They all gave me the thumbs-up signal. Then I stepped into the elevator and watched the doors close behind me.

I stood in that crowded elevator and waited to be caught. Held my breath because I couldn't believe I was there. But no hand grabbed me by the scruff of the neck. No irate guard seized my arm and ordered the elevator to return to the ground floor. Nothing happened other than that we continued upwards in the slow, measured ascent that brings people and supplies to the space station.

I'd been there once on a school outing. I remembered seeing shuttles hanging from every available hook. Every now and then one would break off and seemingly drift to one of the space ships that rested in space far enough out to be safe from earth's gravity.

Now, as I waited to be caught, I looked around, prepared to disappear if a guard came too close. I was so tense that I jumped when a male voice spoke from just behind me. "Are you okay?"

I turned and almost rammed a man in uniform

with enough stripes on his sleeve to make a flag. Whoever he was, he was important, and he was looking at me oddly. I folded, knowing I was caught, hugging my stomach as the futility of my efforts washed over me and made knots of my middle. "I'm sorry. I'm so sorry." I wondered what jail was like and how long I'd be incarcerated.

"Space sickness." He looked me up and down and grabbed the sleeve of a passing stewardess. "Do you have something for space sickness? She's got it bad."

The stewardess handed me a package with two capsules along with a bottle of water. "Take these, they'll fix it." She looked around and frowned. "It'll take a few minutes for them to take effect. You might want to find someplace to sit until they kick in but it seems that all the seats are taken. So good luck." She then continued on her sure-footed way along the swaying elevator.

The security guard watched me swallow the pills and some water, calling after the stewardess, "Will she be all right?"

The stewardess didn't even glance back as she answered. "In a little while." She must have given a thousand people the same pills she'd given me. She left me with the security guard, who now scowled as if wondering why he'd bothered with me to begin with. Because now he was stuck with me.

I struggled against that iron look. "I'll be fine. I just need to sit a while." I looked around. The elevator was jammed with people standing, sitting and leaning into the viewing portals for one last glimpse of Earth. There was hardly room to stand, let alone sit. "Don't worry about me. I'll find a corner."

The scowl grew. He'd made me his business and now he was stuck with me until I got better. I wanted him to go away and he wanted to go away but his conscience wouldn't let that happen. He put one large, competent hand in the small of my back and shoved me through the crowd towards a wall. Then he cleared a space along that wall by waving one arm. That was all it took. People looked at his expression and the stripes on his sleeve and just melted away. Then he slid down the wall and pulled me after him. "This'll have to do."

My problem wasn't space sickness, it was terror but the pills did seem to help. The guard remained beside me with arms folded and a determined expression on his face. He stared into space so angrily that I finally said, "I think I'm okay now."

"Good." But he didn't leave. Instead he turned enough to assess my health, eyes going up and down my body, head to toe and back again, in an impersonal manner. My face and my shaking hands. Then my hair. They stayed on my hair. Everyone notices carrot red hair. "You won't have to worry about sunburn on the Destiny." A feeble attempt at humor.

"That's good." An equally feeble answer. He definitely wasn't the conversational type and I didn't want to talk to anyone in a uniform who could throw me into jail. But he was stubborn. He'd do his job and right then, I was it. He opened his mouth a few times, as if to talk, and then shut it because he didn't know what to say and didn't want to talk and would leave as soon as he knew I wouldn't puke all over him. Until then, he'd stick to me like a burr.

I waited for him to leave. Instead, he inspected my face once more and frowned because I wasn't healthy yet. He cast about for something to say. He'd used up the one thing he knew, the red-head comment, but his job probably required that he be friendly. He finally pointed to the nearest viewing port.

We were high enough that the sky was black and forbidding and I could make out the ships near the space station but I couldn't find the Destiny anywhere. I looked and looked, craning my neck, but I saw nothing.

"Over there." His bark had a military sound to it though he could be a civilian. I didn't know which security was. His black hair was military short, and he had nicely proportioned shoulders and the strong build that seems to be mandatory for all soldier types. So he might be military. Whoever he was, I was screwed if he asked too many questions.

He was pointing to what I'd thought was empty space. I followed his finger to the dim outlines of something so huge my mind had difficulty accepting that it was a ship. It was so black that it was almost lost against the sky. It was miles long and shaped like a cigar. My eyes went wide.

He almost smiled at my expression. Not quite, but almost. "Most people have that reaction when they first see the Destiny." There was pride in his face and in his voice. He loved the huge thing out there.

I had no idea what to say in the face of such pride

because I was terrified of the black space ship but I had to say something. "We're going on an adventure."

I waited for him to laugh at my inane comment. Or leave. He did neither. He stayed beside me, arms folded now that he'd shown me the Destiny, looking over the crowd in the elevator. I began to wonder whether he was sticking to me because he was concerned about my well being or because he suspected something and was merely verifying my guilt.

I needed him gone before I puked from pure fear, but I couldn't very well ask him to leave so I decided to imitate his impersonal behavior and inspect him as he'd inspected me. Maybe he'd be as uncomfortable under my inspection as I was under his. Maybe he'd leave.

As I looked him up and down I decided that under different circumstances I'd be impressed. And interested. He was good looking, though judging by the people in the elevator with us, that was a requirement for being on the Destiny. I'd not seen a homely person yet. Lots of muscles and tons of glowing health. Still, even with glowing health and good looks as common as they seemed to be, the guy beside me stood out from the crowd.

I checked the stripes on his sleeve again. I hoped he wasn't very important but I was afraid he was. If there were any more stripes, he'd need longer arms. "I'm not good at military stuff so I'm sorry to say that I don't recognize your rank."

It was in his long-suffering expression that I should

know his rank, everyone should, which meant he was important. Very important. But all he said was, "I'm in Security."

"Oh." My voice slid up an octave. His job was looking for people like me. I should get away from him as quickly as possible and then I should avoid all further contact with him. But I should do so politely so as not to make him suspicious. So when I was able to make my voice fairly normal, with only a slight squeak, I asked, "Do you like Security?"

As I spoke I inched away, planning to stand up soon, as casually as possible, thank him for helping, say I was fine and look for the nearest group to disappear into. But he didn't seem to know that. He leaned back and gazed at nothing as he thought over my question as if the answer was actually important. "Do I like my job? Yes, I do. It gives me the life I choose."

That stopped me. This ship, this trip was what he wanted out of life? I couldn't believe it. "You prefer a life in space, never to return?"

"Exactly." Seeing my expression, he added, "I like space and I'm not leaving anything important behind." He took a deep breath, realizing I didn't feel the same way and that, somehow, we were in a conversation, so, like it or not, he had to say something. "It's a huge ship. Enough room for ten times the people who are going and I enjoy solitude. I'll get it on the Destiny." His eyes swept over me again and, as the inspection ended, he nodded. I wasn't sick any longer. I wouldn't puke all over him. He could leave. So as soon as possible without looking like he was running away, he nodded politely, rose in one easy movement, and left without looking back.

I watched him disappear into the throng and was careful to avoid anyone in a uniform for the rest of the trip. After many, many hours of slow ascent, we reached the space station. The doors to the airlock opened and we all trudged across the station without being allowed time to gawk as in that school trip, until we were in the airlock that led to the shuttles that would take us to the Destiny.

We weren't counted, and we weren't asked for identification. We were simply herded into a shuttle and told to sit. The shuttle crew looked as if they were tired of ferrying colonists, which they probably were, and were glad we were the last. Doors were locked, the shuttle was disengaged from the station, and we glided across miles of black space to the Destiny.

It was an easy trip. It took mere minutes to go from the known to the unknown. From the life I'd expected to live to one I'd never have chosen if there'd been any choice. As the Destiny loomed larger and larger in the view port, terror started in the pit of my stomach and threatened to keep me glued to my seat. Even the space sickness pills didn't help. I was leaving Earth, leaving home, leaving everything I'd known or hoped to know. I was going into space. Forever.

Chapter Two

When we docked with the Destiny and everyone prepared to leave the shuttle I didn't think I'd be able to stand. I was sure I couldn't follow the other colonists down the aisle. I was positive I couldn't enter the small, round, undulating tube connecting the shuttle to the Destiny and I knew that if I did manage to enter the tube I'd faint before reaching the space ship that hung at the far end.

None of those things happened. I stood up and walked and then I kept on walking. As I entered the gently swaying tube and felt my stomach knotting, a hand appeared from nowhere and braced the center of my back. Just like before. "It's just a short walk." It steered me smoothly but surely through the tube and then into an unremarkable, square room. Gray and unfurnished, it resembled a prison. My first impression of my new home was prison gray. "That wasn't so bad, was it?"

I turned. The security guard with all the stripes on his arm was behind me, pushing me forward, but as soon as we emerged onto the boarding deck of the Destiny, his hand dropped, and he disappeared. Several men and women in uniforms similar to his but with fewer stripes or none at all on their sleeves came up to him with tablets to be signed and questions to be answered. He turned away from me and towards them as if I'd never existed. Thank goodness.

"You've got a friend there." A middle-aged woman, a colonist with two children in tow, had watched me cross with the help of the security guard.

"I suppose so."

"Cullen Vail is head of Security. He's important." She shuddered. "And he doesn't suffer fools at all. I'd hate to be on his bad side."

Fighting sheer terror as I realized I'd been hobnobbing with a man who could put me in prison for the rest of my life with no more than a nod of his head, I rushed after the woman and the other colonists who were disappearing through an open door on the opposite side of the room. But I stole a moment to see if he was watching.

He was. That almost smile ghosted across his face again and sent such a shock through my system that I ended up careening into the back of the nearest colonist who sorely disliked being knocked sidewise by a slip of a redhead. But, with a long-suffering frown, he held his temper and kept the door open until I was though. I heard him mutter something about redheads and why'd they have to be on the Destiny anyway? When I was through he let it slam shut and then he turned away and deliberately ignored me. Good.

I took a second to lean against the wall and breathe a sigh of relief. I was finally beyond notice of the head of Security and I was on the Destiny, the largest space ship ever built, possibly the largest that ever would be built. If I wasn't discovered and sent home in disgrace, I'd soon be heading into deep space and a life I'd never have imagined in my wildest dreams.

No one showed the colonists where to go or gave them any orders, which meant they already knew their way around the Destiny. The media had been full of details of life on the Destiny so I should know all about it but I'd been too busy with finals and orals and writing my doctoral thesis to notice. Now I wracked my brain for any tiny detail I might have noticed on the TV as I passed it on my way to write still another paper.

There were villages, I remembered that much, ten in all with a thousand people in each. That's what they called the clusters of housing units or whatever the colonists and crew lived in. I also knew that babies could only be conceived as space and resources allowed, a necessity on a ship of limited size and capacity though the ship could hold ten times the number of people going into space. They'd deliberately planned for future population growth. Pets, too, were limited, though they were allowed. Food would be grown on the Destiny but I didn't remember where it would be grown or how. Greenhouses? Terrariums? Container gardens? My knowledge was woefully lacking.

I followed the colonists and we all headed for what looked like a huge tube that ran down the center of the ship. I remembered reading that the center tube was the part with no gravity so it was used for transportation among other things. Once in the tube, we all grabbed straps and were pulled along at a decent clip. Most of the tube was opaque, filled with cubicles and offices but every so often we'd pass a clear area.

The first time it happened I almost puked. The ground was miles below. I looked every which way to avoid looking down but even up was down in the tube. The Destiny was huge, ten miles across and fifty miles long. I'd read the numbers but they'd meant nothing to me at the time. Now they did. I swallowed a few times and concentrated on the tube itself and the other colonists and gradually forgot the ground so far below.

We slowed as we reached a tube that branched off from the main one. It was an elevator. A handful of colonists let go of their straps and drifted towards it. Then they punched a button and it started down. But most stayed where they were. Soon we reached a second such tube and more colonists left. They were all headed to their new homes.

If I stayed where I was, I'd end up at the other end of the Destiny and there wouldn't be any more elevators to take me to ground level. I didn't know what might be waiting for me at the end and I didn't want to know, which meant I'd have to pick a village and go down the elevator with a group of colonists. I'd have to pretend I belonged and hope they didn't know the difference.

When we reached the next elevator, I let go of my strap and floated to the elevator along with a few dozen colonists. Rather, I tumbled and was grabbed by a man with a lazy grin who could be my grandfather. "Not got your space legs yet?"

"Nope." I tried to be nonchalant.

"It happens. Took my grandson a while to get his, but he made it." He swung me around and plunked my feet on the floor of the elevator and put my hands on the straps that would keep me from flying aimlessly about until gravity kicked in and kept me in place. I couldn't wait.

He looked like he was enjoying the ride, doing a double somersault before settling down with a strap of his own. He looked like a nice guy. The first I'd met since reluctantly joining the colonists. "You remind me of my grandfather."

"I remind everyone of their grandfather." He grinned again and held out a hand. "Wilkes Zander at your service and I have three real grandkids waiting for me down there and anyone who needs a grandfather can call on me any time."

"I might do that," I managed, figuring out why he was there with other elderly people heading out into space. Remembering something I'd read and not paid attention to at the time. That every family and every colony need grandparents.

As gravity took hold, my stomach settled, and I began to think I had a chance after all. The elevator sides were clear, I could watch the ground rushing towards us and I held my breath because it looked just like home. Like Earth. Green growing things as far as I could see and fruit trees in bloom. It was beautiful.

"Lovely, isn't it?" Wilkes Zander looked proudly

around. "No place on the real Earth is prettier."

"It's just like home."

"It is home, girlie. It's your new home and you'll never be homesick for Earth as long as you're on the Destiny."

All that green would sicken and die if I wasn't there. But I was there so it would remain green and healthy and the colonists would live. I knew that as surely as I knew my own name.

As the elevator hit the ground with a slight bump, Wilkes Zander added, "A few normal trees would be nice, but these bushes are almost as good."

What looked like normal trees from the elevator were actually bushes or dwarf trees. As a botanist I knew they required less food and water and produced just as much fruit or nuts as a normal sized tree and as much oxygen. As I looked around, I realized that every bush or dwarf tree in sight bore something that could be harvested and eaten, as did the very grass that grew along the path that stretched before us. The Destiny was one huge farm. I was sure that there was a blueprint somewhere with every bush and tree on it, along with exactly how much oxygen it should create and how much fruit or nuts it should produce.

I'd make sure that those carefully selected plants would do what they were supposed to do. I'd make sure the harvest was on time and bountiful. I'd keep the food alive that kept the colonists alive even in the dead of outer space. But first I had to find a place to hide.

"You coming?" Wilkes Zander was waiting.

Everyone else had gone on ahead. "We should get going. Check in and do whatever else there is to do." He held out a hand.

I froze. I couldn't check in. But neither could I take a chance and alienate this man. I put my hands on my stomach. "In a little while."

"Still feeling sick?" I nodded. "It takes a while with some people."

I leaned against an apple tree, carefully fitting myself between two low-growing branches. The tree nicely made room for me and I thanked it silently. "I'll be along in a bit. I just need to sit a moment."

"Sure. I understand." He started away. "I, on the other hand, want to get all that paperwork over with, but I'll come back when I'm done to make sure you're okay. You might need to take something for a while. A week or so. My grandson took pills for two weeks before his stomach settled down."

"I'm sure I'll be fine in a few minutes."

"I'll check back anyway. Wouldn't want anyone to be sick when the Destiny gets going. That'll be something. Don't want to miss it."

"Soon?" I pretended interest.

"Don't know when, exactly. It's not as if we are on a schedule. We'll leave when everything is ready. When the countdown is done. Maybe tomorrow, maybe next week. Or maybe tonight. We're all staying up late just in case. Even the kids, we're taking them over to the viewing room. What about you?"

"Sounds like fun."

He looked me over. "You don't look good. Are you

sure you're okay?"

"I look worse then I feel. Don't worry about me." I made a shooing motion. "Go fill out those papers and find your grandkids."

With a guilty look, he took me at my word. "Join us tonight if you feel up to it. Lots of people, good food and drinks." He scampered after the handful of colonists heading towards a nearby cluster of buildings. The village. There was even a sign. New Rochelle. Whoever designed the Destiny went to great lengths to make it resemble a series of rural communities. He waved as he followed the path into the thicket of cherry bushes between New Rochelle and the elevator that was cleverly hidden in an orchard so as to add to the rural feel of the place. "See you."

I took a deep breath and leaned against that dwarf apple tree and wondered what to do next. Then I moved because I was on what was probably a well-traveled path and the last thing I needed was someone else coming along and asking questions. I stepped off the path and into the orchard and started walking.

As soon as I left the path I was surrounded by trees that had to have been planted as soon as that section of the Destiny was closed in from space in order to have grown to their present size. Fruit hung ripe and ready for the picking. I plucked one and knew I'd not starve as long as I could wander around the huge farm that was the Destiny.

I took another step and several cherry bushes closed behind me. I was well hidden. What better place to take stock and plan my next move? And check out whatever Betts had shoved into my pocket back on earth.

I took it out. It was a comunit. I slapped it on the back of my hand. After a few seconds of adjustment, during which it did whatever comunits do, it disappeared, replaced by a tiny, multi-colored tattoo similar to the ones worn by every legitimate person on the Destiny. Small enough that my bare wrist hadn't been noticed but I sighed with relief that I, too, could now pass a close inspection.

The comunit was better than anything I'd ever owned on earth. The Destiny had gotten the best of everything because out there in space, if something went wrong, they'd need the best of the best in order to cope and stay alive. For now, though, with my new and very funky comunit, I could link to the Destiny's mainframe. I relaxed against the tree trunk and pulled up an index of the kind of information I'd need to survive.

First things first. Where was I? Where could I hide best? In moments I realized I was probably already in the best place though I'd have to get water, clothing and other things from the nearby village. New Rochelle.

I decided to sleep in the orchard hidden by thick bushes, but other than that, I'd be well advised to mingle with colonists until they got so used to seeing me that they thought I was one of them. Wilkes Zander already thought I was a colonist. So did the man who hated redheads as did the scary Cullen Vail but Wilkes Zander had invited me to the launch party. It would be wise to accept and begin the process of mingling.

I checked the comunit again. I had time to saunter into New Rochelle, scope it out and hopefully find something to wear. Would I steal from a clothesline? Did they have clotheslines? Somehow I'd have to find party clothes and hopefully, some kind of food other than fruit to still the rumbling in my stomach. Apples and cherries were great but I'd need more than that to be well nourished.

Chapter Three

Once on the path again, it was a short walk to the village. As I stepped from the protective foliage of the orchard I took a deep breath and headed straight to the nearest store as if I had as much right as anyone to go inside. I wouldn't buy anything, of course, but maybe I could figure out where necessities were stored on the Destiny. Then I could return in the night and steal what I needed.

I looked around desperately for Wilkes Zander. If he was around, I wanted to wave and greet him as if I belonged. But he was nowhere to be seen. The only person in sight was a little girl of around six or seven with short, blonde hair. She was sitting on the curb and holding a very fat cat. "Do you want a kitten? Gracie will have some pretty soon." She held the cat towards me and pointed to the cat's stomach. "She's pregnant."

A pet would make hiding more difficult. "I don't think I want one right now." Her face fell so I added, "Maybe next time she has kittens."

Her lower lip trembled. "There won't be a next time. She shouldn't be having kittens now." Her hands trembled to match her quivering lip until she had to drop the cat to her lap. "If I can't find homes for her kittens, they'll have to be … "

"No!" I couldn't believe it. The kittens weren't even born and already they were scheduled for execution. "Why?" But I knew why. Because the Destiny had a policy. One pet per family. No exceptions. "I'm so sorry."

"Please." She held the cat out again, tears wetting her face.

I shook my head. "I can't. I just can't." I felt awful, as if I personally was executing the unborn kittens. "I wish I could."

On impulse I picked up the cat and cuddled her. She was heavy, it wouldn't be long before she gave birth. I sent up a small prayer that all of her kittens would be adopted, then I gave her back to the little girl and went into what passed for a store on the Destiny.

It was more of a supply depot than a store, with racks and shelves of clothing sorted by color, type and size. "Not much variety. I hope they do better when the real storekeepers take over. Whoever chose this stuff didn't have much imagination." The woman who spoke carried an armful of shirts and shorts. She waved her chin towards the little girl with the cat. "I'm sorry Alicia bothered you."

"I just wish I could take one of the kittens. But I'm not settled yet."

"I know how it is. This is a busy time for us all." She smiled, but it was a sad smile. "Maybe by the time the kittens are ready to be adopted, you'll be settled in and will change your mind." I mumbled something and pretended to look for a couple of outfits for myself.

What I really did was watch the woman to see what she did next. She simply went to the touchscreen panel near the door, held out the items so they could be swiped, then she swiped her comunit to identify who got the items, and left.

Perhaps I could get some clothes after all. If the comunit was as good as I thought it might be. Imitating her, I found a couple of outfits in my size. I could have carried my new clothes right past that touchscreen and outside and no one would have known any different. The store was empty, evidently the honor system was being used. But I didn't because I wanted to know how well my fake comunit worked. My family is financially well off so perhaps their money had been put to good use.

So, carrying my own supply of clothes from the store, I imitated that woman and swiped my comunit. I waited for alarms to go off but nothing happened. No blinking red lights appeared. No uniformed policeman came to drag me away to prison. I gave thanks to Betts and vowed to thank her somehow, some day. Then I went outside.

I meandered around the village square, for that's what it was, a precisely laid out park surrounded by supply depots disguised as stores. I entered several. No one was in any of them. In the grocery store, I chose pre-packaged food that I ate in the park sitting on a bench beneath a dwarf peach tree. Then I dropped the empty containers in one of the recycling bins that were everywhere and went in search of the launch party.

My plan was to find a corner in the viewing room

and sit there all night with an expression that said I wasn't up to conversation. I figured it would be understandable in the circumstances. Leaving home never to return. But I'd have made an appearance, I'd have begun the process of becoming a part of the Destiny community.

I headed towards the viewing room buoyed by a decent meal and a shower in the washroom of the Laundromat where I'd changed clothes. I'd hidden the beginnings of a stash of stolen things behind a thick cherry bush in the middle of the apple/cherry orchard that was to become my new home.

I felt optimistic for the first time since entering that elevator, maybe due to decent food in my belly. I lifted my chin and walked towards the viewing room with purpose. I could do this. I could survive on the Destiny. Of course, sleeping might be a bit of a problem. The ground wasn't real earth but was, instead, some kind of manufactured stuff that held roots firmly while providing water and nutrients. Whatever it was, it was hard. Really hard. I'd be lucky to get any sleep at all.

On the other hand, if I could walk into a store and take whatever clothes I needed, why couldn't I also take a mattress, pillow and blanket? I'd seen them through the window of a furniture store. So, as I joined a group of colonists headed towards the viewing room and the party, I tucked a reminder into the back of my mind to wander by the town square when the party ended. When it was late and the town of New Rochelle was deserted. And to steal some bedding.

"I don't believe I know you," a middle-aged man said pleasantly as we ended up walking beside each other. My face went stiff.

"She lives around here somewhere," a woman replied. The same woman whose daughter was trying to give away kittens. "I saw her earlier."

What to say? As it turned out, it didn't matter. His attention had turned, albeit unwillingly, to an eloquent plea by a small girl to adopt an unborn kitten. The tiny blonde didn't stop talking until he agreed to take one. As she skipped ahead, having achieved her objective, he simply shook his head and rolled his eyes at me. Then someone beside him spoke, he spoke back, and then he forgot I existed.

By the time we entered the viewing room, more people had joined our group. We were a small crowd as we walked into that place and I was glad because there's safety in numbers. I looked like I belonged.

I looked around for Wilkes Zander and found him on a couch surrounded by several kids. The little girl with the kittens to give away broke free of her mother and ran to him. He gathered her in his arms and lifted her high in the air. She gave shriek of delight then fell into his lap and proceeded to tell him that she'd found a home for another kitten.

Then he noticed me. He waved me over and I went gratefully because, being with him, being with anyone specific, was a sign that I belonged. That someone knew me as a colonist. The couch and surrounding floor were filled with kids so I pulled up a nearby chair and settled down to watch the Destiny depart from as close to Wilkes Zander as possible.

If it left. If the countdown went smoothly.

It must have done so because in less than an hour, as if on cue, we saw the space beyond the viewing ports shift slightly. Nearby ships appeared to move, inches at first, then more and more until it was clear to all of us that we were the ones who were moving even though there was no sensation of motion.

"See, kids. I told you it would be okay. You didn't have to brace yourselves." Wilkes Zander stood up on one foot to prove that the Destiny was stable. Then he threw a handful of candies into the small crowd and left them in order to join the grownups. He waved me along and I followed. "I didn't get your name earlier."

"Elle." I wasn't sure whether I should give my right name because I didn't know if the comunit had been assigned to my cousin Betts or whether it would accept the name of whomever used it. But I had to say something. I decided that if there were questions I'd say Elle was my middle name and I'd used it without thinking, though if that happened I'd probably be in jail and they'd already know all about me.

There were no crew members in the viewing room, nor were there any security personnel. I asked Wilkes about it. "Too busy. There's hundreds of ships out there saying goodbye and the Destiny is huge. The captain doesn't want any collisions."

"But where are the security guards?"

"They are around. You may not notice them but they are everywhere." I shivered. "You see them now and then." His eyes gleamed. "You're looking for Cullen

Vail, aren't you?" I informed him that the head of Security was none of my concern but he waved aside my protests. "Nice guy, Cullen, though a bit on the stuffy side and he'd make a good hermit." He inspected me carefully as if wondering what Cullen Vail saw in me. "Unless some woman gets her hands on him and changes that." I told Wilkes that Cullen had dealt with my stomach ache and couldn't get away fast enough. He laughed, not believing a word. "I wish you luck if he's what you're looking for. You'll need it."

Someone produced pop and cupcakes and in a corner there were stronger beverages. Soon the party went viral, with music and dancing and if there'd been an empty table, someone would have been on it. I drank only pop because I couldn't take a chance on getting tipsy though I gobbled enough cupcakes to go a week without food. Then I found a couch as far away from the viewing windows as possible and tried hard not to cry. Unlike everyone else in the room, I didn't want to watch my home slipping inexorably away.

Eventually the party ended, as much from sheer weariness as because anyone had to be at work in the morning. "Good thing tomorrow is Saturday," someone commented. Someone else answered, "I'll be way too wasted in the morning to go to work." And a third put in, "Shouldn't this become a holiday? Destiny Day or something like that? The day we started the journey of a lifetime." There were cheers and whistles and someone said they'd bring it up at the next village meeting.

No work tomorrow? That meant colonists had

jobs. Just like home. I decided to wander into town Monday morning to see where they went. I should figure out a way to look as if I, too, had a job like everyone else. Then I pretended to fall asleep as the party wound down.

After the last colonist had tiptoed softly past in order not to wake me and disappeared down the path towards New Rochelle, I rose quietly and followed at a good distance. By the time I reached the town square, it was deserted with the exception of one figure in the darkness. I eased behind a store and waited for him to go home. He didn't.

I squinted. Darn. It was Cullen Vail, pacing steadily back and forth. Making his rounds. Keeping New Rochelle safe from felons like me. I dropped to my knees behind a voluminous raspberry bush by the store wall and waited for him to leave, which he did after a few moments.

When I was sure he was gone, I slipped into a store and pulled a lightweight mattress, a pillow and a blanket from the shelves and then dragged them into the apple-cherry orchard. I was glad for the artificial dirt because I left no trace behind. But when I was getting ready to turn the mattress into a bed, something stopped me. A sound.

I froze. Dropped to the ground and lay as still as possible as I waited to be uncovered. I was afraid to look towards the sound, afraid to make any movement at all, so I just lay and waited to be caught. To be imprisoned. The be thrown out the airlock.

Those are the things I expected to happen.

Instead, I heard music. The clear, lovely sound of pan pipes drifted towards me through the night air. I'd heard them before. One of my aunts had whittled a set from reeds growing near her home and bound them together with twine. When she was finished, she'd winked at me and played a melody. I danced and after that I danced every time she played them because she played happy music.

The songs I heard now were hauntingly beautiful. I couldn't decide whether they were happy or sad because, in a way I couldn't fathom, they were both. I wondered who was making such music and what led to the choice of songs. Was the musician pouring out what he was feeling, what everyone was most likely feeling beneath the public gaiety, as the Destiny headed out of the solar system?

I crawled on my belly without a sound through the cherry bushes until I could make out a form in the dimness that passed for night on the space ship. No moon because there was no need for one. But the darkness was a good imitation of night. It was almost like nights on earth when the moon was new but stars were bright though instead of stars the night sky on the Destiny was a bluish, filtered glow. In that faint light I could vaguely make out the musician's form but not well enough to recognize it. I scrabbled back to my cherry bushes. Then I settled down to listen.

The concert went on for what I judged to be the better part of an hour. Then, abruptly, the musician rose and left. He passed within two feet of my hiding spot but the bushes were thick and he saw nothing. I said a prayer of thanks for my invisibility even as I wished I could tell him how much I liked his music. How it reminded me of my aunt's songs. But speaking would be suicide and in moments he was gone.

I crawled to my mattress, slid onto it, pulled the blanket over me, shoved my face into the pillow and eventually fell asleep, the first night of my new, unplanned life. But the lovely melodies of pan pipes floated through my sleep and were a comforting counterpart to dreams of the formidable, sculpted face and shoulders of Cullen Vail. In my dreams, his figure was intimidating and frightening as we headed away from everything I'd ever known. But because of that unknown musician those dreams were interspersed with the memory of beautiful music. I clung to those remembered notes because somehow I knew they'd keep me sane in this new, totally insane life.

Chapter Four

I hung around the apple orchard Saturday and Sunday, exploring and getting to know the trees, bushes and other growing things. Monday, after a breakfast of cherries and apples I set off for New Rochelle to see what a day in the life of a colonist was like so as to better know how to imitate that life. What I found was an almost empty square. Only one person was in sight. The little girl with the kittens, in the same place as before, holding her very pregnant cat and trying to find homes for the unborn kittens. She saw me and waved. "Can you take a kitten yet?"

I dropped to the curb beside her. It felt right to do so. In fact, it felt more like the small town I'd grown up in than a gigantic space ship. The designers were geniuses. In a few days I'd forget that I wasn't really in a peaceful farming community. "Not yet."

"I saw you at the party." She looked me up and down. "My name's Alicia."

I held out my hand. "Elle."

"I know. I heard you tell my grandfather."

"Wilkes Zander is your grandfather?'

"He's also the Mayor of New Rochelle." She cuddled her cat. "He's important." She stroked the cat and it purred loudly. "But not important enough to save the extra kittens if I can't find homes for all of them."

"I'm sure you'll find homes for every one of them."

"If you take one I'll bring food every day."

I sighed, stroking the cat's plush fur. "I wish I could. I had a cat when I was a kid. But I can't right now."

"She was pregnant when we moved here. I sneaked her on board. She'll be fixed after the kittens come so she won't be a problem after that." To Alicia, boarding the Destiny was as simple as a move to a new town. "I didn't see you yesterday. Do you live in an apartment? We live in a big one."

I stopped petting the cat and rose slowly so the movement would seem casual but I wanted to get away before she asked a question I couldn't answer. This little girl who talked nonstop asked a lot of questions. "Yes. That's where I live." What excuse would get me away? "I should go now and get to work."

"Everyone else went to work hours ago." She looked at me suspiciously.

"Not that kind of work. I meant that I need to unpack. Boxes all over the place." She understood that and nodded, bending her head over her cat. I started away. Then I stopped and changed my mind about leaving. Perhaps I could ask questions of this child that would arouse suspicion if asked of an adult. "What do your parents do? What kind of work? Maybe I work with them."

"They're farmers. Almost everyone in New Rochelle is a farmer. Aren't you a farmer?"

"Uh... yes." How to defuse the suspicion beginning in her eyes? "A special kind of farmer. I'm a botanist."

"What kind of farmer is that?"

"It means I went to school to learn farming."

"My family didn't have to go to school. They just know how."

"Good for them."

"Were you harvesting apples in the orchard?"

My heart began thudding in my chest. This small child knew where I was from. My safety was already compromised. Worse, if all of the residents of New Rochelle were farmers, how long would it be before they harvested the apples and uncovered my hiding spot? "I wasn't harvesting them, not yet. I was checking on them. They are coming nicely. Almost ripe."

Alicia looked at me as if I was an idiot and it hit me. Of course! The trees had blossoms and green fruit and ripe apples all at the same time so fruit could be harvested continuously. Genetic manipulation at work. "I mean there are a lot ready right now. Enough that it'll be worth harvesting them any day now. I enjoy harvesting. Do you?"

She nodded and pointed to a building across the square that looked just like all the other buildings in the village. "Did you sign up yet? You have to sign up before anyone else if you want to harvest the apples in that orchard."

I gave Alicia her cat, fighting excitement. Could I

harvest them? If so, I could protect my hiding place and look like I had a legitimate job at the same time. It was almost too good to be true. "I forgot. Guess I should go now and sign up." I sauntered across the park to the building she'd indicated, moving casually so she wouldn't be suspicious. But it was hard, I wanted to run.

The inside of the building resembled any government facility everywhere. Touch-screens everywhere, bulletin boards with papers pinned to them and a couple of library tables and chairs. I'd dealt with the government enough during my graduate days to find my way around with no trouble so soon I was signed up to single-handedly harvest all the apples and cherries in the orchard near New Rochelle. Thank goodness no one had already claimed them.

When I left, my name was on one more official Destiny list, just as if I was a genuine colonist and I could be fairly sure that my hiding place was safe since I was the only person harvesting anything in that particular area. I'd held my breath while flashing the comunit tattoo across the screen because I used my real name but Elle Olmstead still raised no red flags in the Destiny's database.

When I came back outside, Alicia and her cat were gone, and the square was deserted. Deciding I'd accomplished enough for the moment I took a shower in the Laundromat bathroom as I waited for my clothes to get clean. As I dried myself, I took a long look at my reflection in the tiny mirror above the sink and did some serious thinking.

I'd gotten on the Destiny because I resembled a family of redheads but now that I was on board that resemblance could work against me. What if someone asked the family about me and they said they had no such daughter? What if I happened to be in the same place as that family and they denounced me? What then?

So when I was dry and dressed I headed to the grocery store and filled a bag with more than groceries. I carried everything back to the cherry bushes. Digging in the bag, I pulled out the mirror and scissors from the grocery store personal products aisle. Then I cut my hair.

When I was done, I combed brown dye from that same store through what hair was left. There was nothing I could do about the curls and I didn't dare dye my hair too dark because my few acquaintances already knew me as a redhead. But when I looked in that mirror once more, the red in my hair was muted. I wasn't a carrot top. I'd no longer be taken as a member of that family. I sighed in relief. I had a place to live, my name didn't send up red flags when I used my comunit and I was now myself instead of a member of a family that could out me.

I decided it was time to find out about this new home of mine that was whizzing through space at frightening speed. The Destiny had a full library accessible to anyone with a comunit, though some subjects were restricted to crew members with special access codes. I didn't care about those parts, I wanted to learn about every day life. So I leaned against a tree trunk and took a crash course on how to be a colonist. Among other things, I learned the proper process for harvesting apples and cherries. I vowed to do it right, to not arouse suspicion.

Using my new-found information, a few days later I went to the nondescript building in New Rochelle that I now knew was the harvesting center and picked up a cart and tractor. A half hour later, the wagon was full of cherries and apples, but one of the first things I'd learned as a child was not to show off my abilities. I waited until evening to bring the full wagon back to the center. I spent the intervening time checking out the trees and bushes. They were growing nicely and would fill another cart with produce the next day if I wanted them to. But I didn't. That would be too soon.

At the harvesting center, the wagon was quickly unloaded, and my paperwork processed. Nothing aroused the suspicion of the clerk who didn't even look at me as he waved me off, eager to get to the next person and be done for the day.

Soon I settled into the same routine as the legitimate colonists. I had a job and I made sure that I did it openly and properly. I procured groceries at the store and washed my clothes at the Laundromat, though I only did so when it was empty so as not to call attention to the fact that I also showered there instead of at home like everyone else.

And I listened to the music of pan pipes occasionally at night, though I never discovered the identity of the piper beyond the fact that it was a man. A large man who moved through the trees and bushes as stealthily as a cat when the music was done and it was time to leave. He never took the same route out of the orchard twice and that bothered me. He could stumble onto my hideout.

With that in mind, one day I dragged the mattress and my few possessions deeper among the cherry bushes before leaving with my harvest. When I returned the bushes had grown tightly around my things, encircling them with a wall of greenery so thick no one could find me unless they knew where to look.

The next time the piper came in the middle of the night, I lay back without fear of discovery and let myself enjoy the music as I regained the sanity I was in danger of losing because I didn't truly know how to be a fugitive. The music was enough like my aunt's songs that it reminded me that I was a worthwhile human being after all and I was mentally transported back to Earth and my home. I soon felt tears coursing down my cheeks. The thick greenery muffled the sound of my sobbing. I was grateful.

During the daytime it was easy to forget that I was a fugitive. I came to like the area and the people who lived there. I was happy, and it was only at night when the music of the mysterious piper took me back home that I cried. During the day, I could almost believe I was back on Earth just outside the small town where I grew up. I'd always thought my family lived in the most perfect place possible.

Because of that upbringing, I knew how small towns worked and I also knew that the Destiny was organized around a rural governmental system. I used that information and that knowledge to blend in.

I used my comunit freely now that I knew the Destiny communications systems accepted it as valid. I talked with people I met on the street though I never gave them a chance to ask personal questions. I became a member of the community.

That first week soon became another, and another, until almost two months passed. I began to think that the whole stowaway thing might work. I relaxed somewhat and only then did I realize how tense I'd been. When the mysterious piper came in the middle of the night, the music was so relaxing that one night I fell asleep in the middle of a song and had no idea when he left.

I grew so bold that I didn't panic when Cullen Vail, the man who could throw me out of an airlock, appeared, though I would have avoided him if possible. I ran into him at the New Rochelle café, a place I'd carefully avoided whenever anyone wearing a Security uniform was around, but twice Cullen Vail came in when I was already there and filling my plate. I couldn't very well drop it and run because I saw him.

When I turned around to look for an empty table, there he was, less than three feet away, filling his own plate. Lasagna and an apple, probably one from my trees. His uniform stood out in that place of casual dress.

We stared at each other too long to pretend we didn't recognize each other. His scowl, followed by a fake smile, told me he didn't want to talk to me any more than I wanted a conversation with him. But his job required that he be friendly, I'd read that in the Destiny library. Security was to keep people safe not to scare them and Cullen Vail wanted to be the perfect security person so if being friendly was part of the job then he'd be friendly or die in the attempt.

He smiled but it didn't reach his eyes. "Got your space legs yet?"

I looked for somewhere else to be than beside him and saw an empty table against the wall. I slid sidewise around his uniformed bulk and headed towards that table, tossing a reply back over my shoulder. "I'm fine thank you." I sat down and didn't look at him again, knowing he didn't want to be with me either, though I watched him from the corner of my eye.

When his own plate was full he joined Alicia and her family, sitting beside Wilkes Zander, the mayor of New Rochelle. He was here on business. Nothing to do with me. All I had to do was get out of there as fast as possible. I gobbled my lunch and in minutes I was back among my nice, safe cherry bushes.

The second time I saw him things went down a bit differently. As I filled my plate, Alicia and her mom waved to me from a table in the middle of the room. "Come on over and join us."

I did as they asked and, as soon as I saw who was at the table, I wished I'd not taken them up on their offer, but I'd already started in their direction so I was stuck. Worse, there was only one empty seat so I had to take it. Next to Cullen Vail, of course. Alicia's mother caught my expression as I eyed him. "Do you two know each other?"

Cullen Vail gave me the kind of look usually reserved for pythons. My arm brushed his and we both jumped as if shot. Alicia's mother's eyebrows rose but she said nothing and Alicia chatted away in blissful ignorance of the tension that suddenly appeared. Cullen muttered something about having met once or twice, and then he shut up.

"The kittens are old enough to leave home," Alicia said, looking meaningfully at both Cullen and me but she focused mainly on me. "Are you ready for a kitten yet? They are born and there's one left."

"I'm so sorry, but I can't."

Temporarily giving up on me, she skewered Cullen with a look. "What about you?"

It was easy to see that he was afraid of children, but he managed to come up with an answer. "My job doesn't allow for pets. I'm gone a lot."

Her shoulders slumped and her eyes teared as her mother hugged her. "Honey, I'm sure someone will want the kitten. We'll find a home for it. There's still time."

Alicia put her head in her mom's shoulder and sobbed briefly. Then she pulled back and stared long and hard at Cullen and me again as she let us know what she wanted, saying pointedly, "Yes. We. Will. Find. It. A. Home."

Cullen Vail avoided her stare by turning towards Wilkes Zander and soon the two men were discussing the politics of New Rochelle. I listened while pretending not to, knowing this was a business meeting disguised as lunch and, since I was already committed to being a part of the group, I wanted to gather as much information as possible. Some tidbit might help me avoid capture. But all they did was talk about people they knew and soon Cullen Vail excused himself and left.

When Cullen Vail was gone Wilkes Zander shook his head, grinning widely. "That's it for two weeks."

"Huh?" I didn't understand.

"There are ten villages on the Destiny. Wilkes Zander has lunch in one of the villages every week day. He pretends to be visiting but he's checking us out." Everyone at the table laughed, this was an old joke. "Ten villages means two weeks. So he'll be back after visiting the other villages. In two weeks."

I thought back to the last time I'd met him in the café. It had likely been two weeks ago. I checked the calendar, now knowing when not to eat in town.

As soon as was decent, I told everyone at the table that I had work to do, and left. It was all I could do not to run through town and into the apple orchard. I didn't stop shaking until I was safely surrounded by the cherry bushes and apple trees that folded themselves around me and hid me from the world.

When I stopped shaking, I examined the orchard. The apples were growing their little hearts out but I'd brought a cart full to town earlier that day along with cherries that were so abundant that I'd suggested they slow down a bit, after thanking them for doing so well, of course. It happens that way sometimes in my family. Things grow better than they ever did before. We are good at what we do. But I shouldn't take another load of fruit to town for a few days. Maybe a week.

So, with nothing to do in the orchard and not daring to show up in town in case Cullen Vail was still there, I decided to take a nap but it took long minutes to slip into slumber because I was already rested and was still somewhat nervous from the fright I'd had in the cafe. I lay with my eyes shut tightly.

Then my skin prickled because someone was looking at me. CullenVail? Had he followed me from the village? But I couldn't keep my eyes closed forever. I had to face the music some time, so I opened them. And saw Alicia holding a kitten and staring down at me.

I sat up fast.

She held the kitten out. It was nothing special, black and gray mottled. Just a kitten, but she loved it. "I thought that since you're hiding, maybe you'd hide my kitten too."

"Hiding?" I gulped. "I'm not hiding."

"Yes, you are. I know you are. I've been watching you. You come here all the time, you tell stuff to grow and it does, then you tell it to jump into the cart and it does, and you don't have an apartment after all." Blue eyes drilled holes into me. "I figure you ran away from home. Was it bad there? Mom says people do that sometimes and it's okay if it was bad."

"Uh..." I thought hard. "Yes. I did. I ran away." She was a kid, she didn't realize that making things grow by telling it to do so was unusual. "But not because it was bad. Because ..." I thought hard. "Because I wanted to be in the orchard."

She nodded. "Sometimes I want to run away but

I'm not old enough." She dropped the kitten into my lap. It was small and soft and mewed in fright. Instinctively I picked it up and cuddled it. Alicia's face glowed brightly. "You like him, and he likes you. You can keep him."

"I can't ... "

"I'll bring food. I promise. I won't forget, not ever." She hopped from one foot to the other. "I've got to go before my mom comes looking for me. She doesn't know I'm here, she thinks I'm in the field."

I couldn't have her mother come to my hideout. "Yes, you should go." The small thing in my arms licked my face. "I'll keep the kitten." I was desperate for Alicia to leave before she led someone to my hideout. "I'll hide it for you." I stared at it eyeball to eyeball as it mewed softly. "What's its name?"

"It's a boy kitten and it doesn't have a name yet." She was gone and I was left with one small kitten and the knowledge that my hiding place wasn't so secret after all. Alicia knew about it. Did anyone else? Fear curled around my stomach and I hugged the tiny kitten for comfort and was glad for his warm body against mine.

We were both outcasts and both in danger of being executed if we were caught. "Well, kitten." I stared at him. "I guess it's you and me now whether it's what we want or not." He mewed his agreement and I put him on the mattress where he curled against me. "Don't worry little guy. I'll protect us. We'll be just fine." I hoped we'd be fine.

Saying the words made my plight real and more

dangerous than I'd been willing to admit. I laid a hand on his tiny back. "Don't be afraid." He wasn't afraid. In fact, he yawned and went to sleep. "Sure. Sleep away. Don't worry about a thing." He snuggled closer to me and began to snore gently. "You're braver than I am." So I decided to call him Braveheart.

That night the piper came again to unknowingly serenade me. I held my breath, afraid Braveheart would start meowing and, thus give away my hideout. But I held him close and he snuggled in and closed his eyes and listened along with me. My musician ... for that was how I'd come to think of him ... was none the wiser.

The next day I didn't know what to do with Braveheart when I brought my weekly load of apples to town so I brought him with me, tucked in a pocket. The man at the depot took time to pet him. "You're the sucker who got him, eh? I told Alicia she'd find someone to take him." He held the kitten high and scratched it under its chin. "Nice kid, Alicia, even if she is a bit of a busybody." I giggled because he'd described her perfectly. "Her grandfather is the village mayor so I guess she comes by it naturally." He doubled over laughing along with me.

I had lunch at the café, not staying long enough for anyone to ask too many questions, then, after stopping at the store for cat food and other cat necessities, I made my way back to my homey cherry bushes. I looked around and wondered if I dared bring a chair back the next time I was in town. The mattress was nice but a chair would be pure luxury.

I poured cat litter into the pan from the store, then I looked around for a private place to put Braveheart's bathroom. I parted a pair of bushes. And found myself looking at a pair of small, bare feet. I sighed. "Alicia, what are you doing here? Don't you know that it's hard to keep a hiding place secret if people come all the time?"

"I brought cat food." She held out a small package. "I said I would."

I was about to say that I'd already gotten food for Braveheart when a sound stopped me. Stopped us both. Froze us like statues because someone was approaching along the same path Alicia had used. I said a prayer and waited for Cullen Vail to arrest me.

Instead, Wilkes Zander parted the bushes and stared at the tableau before him. His granddaughter, a kitten, a mattress that was neatly made up for sleeping, and me. "What have we here?" was all he said in a deceptively mild voice as he took in my horrified expression. "And why is someone living in the apple orchard?"

I tried to speak and failed. I tried again, but before I could get a word out ... before I could figure out what to say, even ... Alicia spoke. "She's hiding. She ran away."

Wilkes Zander blinked but said nothing for a long-drawn-out moment. In that moment a thousand thoughts chased each other across his face. He was everyone's grandfather, he was a nice guy, but he was no fool and there was a reason he'd been elected mayor of New Rochelle. The moment he saw me and my hideout, he knew I was a stowaway.

Braveheart mewed and went to him. The kitten knew him, Wilkes had probably played with him while visiting Alicia. Now Alicia spoke, as usual. "Elle is taking the kitten. Now they all have homes."

Wilkes' eyes narrowed, and he looked at me and then they swerved to Alicia. He loved his granddaughter dearly and he knew what would happen to Braveheart if I went to jail. The kitten would be executed ,and Alicia would be devastated and she'd blame him.

He couldn't let that happen. He lifted his eyes to the fake sky as if seeking Devine guidance. Then he spoke, still in that mild tone of voice that hid the steel of his being that I hadn't known existed until that moment. "I think it's time to stop hiding, Elle." He stared at my newly muted red hair. "I understand why you might not want to live with your family any longer." He picked his way through a morass of possible things to say and he did so carefully. He didn't want Alicia to know the truth about me or about what he was about to do. Which was?

I held my breath. "Elle, I understand that you want to live on your own. But you shouldn't have run away to the forest. You could have asked me for an apartment. I'd have made sure you got something decent and I'd have done so without anyone else being involved." He paused and then, so there'd be no mistaking his meaning, he added, "We can take care of it now if you wish. If you want an apartment like everyone else on the Destiny. Just you and me, we don't need any help."

It was almost a minute before I could speak well enough to reply. "Thank you." He tipped his head and stared at me hard. The friendly eyes were still friendly but they were also granite. He was giving me a gift and I'd better not make him regret it. "Thank you, Wilkes. You won't be sorry."

He looked again at my little domicile. "Bring this stuff to town later. Tonight." When no one would notice and ask questions. "We can get the paperwork done now, though, and find you a nice place." He smiled at Alicia and the granite disappeared. He loved his granddaughter dearly. "The kitten can come too, of course."

Alicia hugged her grandfather and I stuffed the kitten back into my pocket as we all headed to town. As we emerged from the apple orchard, he made the laconic comment that there were some perks to being the mayor of New Rochelle.

By evening, I had a furnished apartment. Wilkes Zander's eyes had widened when he tried to give me a comunit and I said I didn't need one. "I've got one already. Doesn't everyone on the Destiny have one?"

"Yes, of course." His expression said that someday he'd ask how I'd gotten something no one on earth had access to. I wondered if I'd ever feel comfortable enough to give him an answer. "Of course, you have a comunit. Of course, you do. You're a colonist." He checked the database and found that I'd been using it regularly and that puzzled him even more. "I'd get that mattress out of the apple orchard as soon as possible if

I were you without making it look like you've been living there." Then he took Alicia and left. I collapsed on the couch of my new home, Braveheart climbed onto my lap and I looked around, daring to breathe at last.

There was a screen on the wall. It was now possible to communicate with friends and relatives on earth until the space ship got so far out in space that the time delay between questions and answers would make even time-delayed conversations not practical. Then electronic letters would be the only option. I'd had no way to access the communication system with earth before getting the apartment so I'd had no way to tell my family how I was doing.

I decided against contacting them face to face the first time we communicated. Their expressions might give me away. Instead I sent a text message to my cousins and even then I was careful about the wording in case messages were vetted by someone on the Destiny. I told them that I was now a resident of New Rochelle and everything was as going as planned. I knew they'd get the general idea and would fill in the blanks. Then I sat back and waited for them to contact me. They did so by Skype less than half an hour later and they were just as careful about what they said as I'd been though it was clear that there were a million questions they'd ask if they could.

My next message was carefully thought out. "The mayor got me an apartment. He's very understanding." When they got that message, their reply was nods to indicate that they knew what I was really saying.

After another delay and another response on their part, I added, "I like New Rochelle. My comunit works everywhere on the Destiny so he didn't have to get me a new one." Betts' imperceptible nod much later said she understood that I'd found the comunit she'd stuck in my pocket and that I'd made good use of it. "So things are going along. The only negative is that I miss you guys. I wish you were here."

When it was their turn again, they said fervently that they wished the same thing and then it was time to end the conversation though we could have talked forever if we could have spoken freely. We promised to talk again and all said goodbye and I was left staring at blank walls.

I went to a window and pulled the curtain aside and was glad that it overlooked a field beside the apple-cherry orchard instead of the town square. I could almost pick out the patch of cherry bushes that I'd thought would be my home forever. I was glad I wasn't there. The apartment was way more comfortable then a mattress on fake dirt and the bathroom was much appreciated, especially the shower. No more laundromat showers for me. And Braveheart loved his new home.

Chapter Five

The apartment was wonderful in that it made it relatively easy to avoid people who might ask embarrassing questions though I did miss sleeping surrounded by beautiful, friendly apple trees that made me feel safe and loved and cherry bushes that hovered over me protectively. I would have been happy there, but I was glad to be a part of the community.

Now, emboldened by this step towards a legitimate existence, I wandered the New Rochelle town square daily, ate occasionally in the café, and made sure to visit for a while with the other farmers when I brought in my weekly harvest of cherries and apples. And I was very careful not to come more than once a week. That seemed appropriate, judging from how often the other farmers brought their own produce in.

Someday, I told myself, I'd be able to do more than live on the fringes of this small town society. Someday I'd be able to have friends. When enough time had passed that earth was merely a place we all had lived at one time, I'd be able to join in the conversations in the town square without worrying about whether the subject of how we came to be on the Destiny came up.

Someday, perhaps, conversations would have moved on to other things. Just in case that never happened, however, I was thinking up a plausible story of my origins that would be accepted. So, even as I worked out a logical story, I merely skimmed the surface of daily life in New Rochelle and stayed home a lot.

I missed the pan pipes. As I lay in my comfortable bed in my lovely bedroom in my decent apartment, I wondered about the man who played such beautiful music. Who was he? Did he miss Earth? Most of all, why did he sneak out to play in the middle of an apple orchard instead of playing where people could enjoy his music?

Though I became a part of the community, I went to great lengths to avoid detection. One thing that helped was the informal dress code everyone had adopted. Most colonists and crew wore shorts and tee shirts and whatever shoes they liked or none at all. When a uniform appeared it stood out. Since it obviously belonged to someone on official business, I simply disappeared whenever I saw someone in long, dark blue pants and a shirt or jacket with precise creases. I scooted around the nearest corner and then made my way back to my apartment where I remained until the uniform was gone. It worked and as weeks passed I became more and more confident of success.

I tried to keep track of the time I'd been on the Destiny, the amount of time that I'd escaped detection, but it became difficult because the more time passed the more it became oddly meaningless. We were there for the duration of the trip and that would be close to a hundred years. Most of us would die of old age on the Destiny.

I only remembered time passing and the ever-widening distance from earth when I spoke with my family. I was glad my parents were no longer alive because there was no despair for leaving them. That had already happened. And I had no siblings, just cousins.

My extended family didn't want to lose me or I them because we all knew that what I was doing was important and they didn't want to diminish that fact or belittle what I was doing. But our lives were now so different that we found less and less to talk about during our disjointed, time-delayed conversations. I now lived at the slow pace of village life while they, some of the best botanists on earth, were in high demand. They were busy people.

Our conversations dwindled to occasional duty calls to make sure I was okay, and I always was. Then one day they missed their usual time and I didn't mind because I didn't know what I'd say to them any more than they knew what to say to me. After that, our conversations dried up and stopped.

I was almost glad because I was becoming involved in my new life in spite of my intention to remain aloof. I didn't even feel like a felon any longer. I felt like I belonged.

One day I awoke to discover that to my surprise I

liked living on the Destiny even though the dirt wasn't real, and it never rained because rain doesn't fall correctly where gravity is weird. And I came to believe, along with my neighbors, that New Rochelle was the best and most wonderful of all the villages on the Destiny.

One morning, after finishing a book from the electronic library, I found myself debating whether to chance lunch in the café or stay in my apartment. It had been two weeks since Cullen Vail's last visit and he was a man of routine so he'd likely return today but I was getting tired of worrying about being discovered. It hadn't happened yet, and I wanted out of my apartment. It wasn't exactly small but that day I was restless, and it felt tiny.

A solution occurred to me. I didn't have to eat in the café. I could eat elsewhere. I didn't have to be a creature of habit. And I like eating outside. So thinking, I packed a picnic lunch and headed to the empty field that was between my apartment building and the apple orchard. It was just beyond my window and a fair number of kids and adults played impromptu baseball games there.

There was no game at the moment so it was peaceful and quiet. Almost like a summer's day on earth. The only thing missing was the sound of insects, but the warmth pouring from the fake sky was the same, never mind that it was precisely programmed for maximum benefit to crops and people. It was perfect and relaxing. I leaned back and closed my eyes and didn't want to be anywhere else in the universe. I wondered if I'd have the energy to open my lunch.

"Hello."

My eyes flew open. It was Cullen Vail himself. My worst nightmare. Two weeks since his last visit. Damn. I should have stayed indoors. I gulped. "Hello."

"I've been looking for you."

Don't arrest me, not here, not now. Not in this lovely place. But all I said was, "Oh?"

He squatted beside me. Folded himself down in a well-practiced manner, then dropped to the ground and stuck long legs in front of him and somehow kept his dignity the whole time. He was both agile and in shape. "I'm here to apologize to you on behalf of the Destiny."

"Huh?" It was all I could manage and, though I wanted to be unfazed by his unexpected appearance, I couldn't stop that single, surprised word from coming out.

"I'm sorry that you didn't have an apartment when you first boarded. That was inexcusable."

I gulped. How'd he learned about the apartment? Then I knew. Wilkes Zander, of course. "There's no need to apologize."

He smiled, a small smile but it was genuine. A first. "Wilkes Zander told me everything. I understand why you took things into your own hands when you decided to move out of your parents' home. He said that you would have moved into an apple orchard if he hadn't intervened. I'm glad it didn't happen, no thanks to the Destiny. We are grateful to Wilkes for taking care of things."

Wilkes hadn't told him everything. Just enough to cover my sudden appearance. "It's a nice apartment."

"One of the smaller ones." He shifted. His leg brushed mine. I had the wild thought that it might just be the first time the head of Security had touched another human being since childhood. Then I discarded the thought as unworthy of me as he continued. "There are larger apartments. You should have something nice. To make up for our inattention." He shifted to better see what I thought of his suggestion.

"No new apartment. The one I have is fine. I like it. In fact I love it."

His eyes narrowed, and our looks met. Clashed. His was smoke and wildfire now that I looked deep into his eyes. How'd I ever thought of him as distant and cold? He wasn't, what I'd seen as lack of emotion was control. The fires were banked but they were there. I didn't know what he saw in my eyes, didn't want to know.

"Are you sure it's sufficient? I've never been in the smaller units but from what I've been told, they are hardly more than one-room efficiencies." He shuddered. "No one should have to live in cramped quarters, not on a life-time trip such as we're on." His shoulders convulsed a second time. It was clear that Cullen Vail had lived in a small space at one time. How small? When? Why?

He recovered his composure quickly and his voice softened, becoming a musical baritone. It was the first time I'd heard him speak without consciously playing the part of a friendly Security guard. "I'll get you a new place immediately."

"I don't want a new place."

"As far as I'm concerned, the small units should be eliminated or combined into larger ones. I've talked with Wilkes Zander about it but he doesn't agree."

"Because he knows they are large enough."

We stared at each other again. Smoke and fire. Inwardly, I shuddered. I didn't want that fire directed at me in anger. "You said you've never seen the small units?"

"Not yet but I know what small living quarters are like."

"Come." I rose and held out my hand to help haul him up but he ignored me and flowed upward in one smooth, incredibly well-coordinated movement. "I'll show you."

He didn't know how to refuse. I saw in his eyes that he wanted to but there was that rule about being friendly and he wasn't sure how it applied in this situation. He indicated that I go ahead and he'd follow.

The apartment wasn't far, nothing was far from anything else in New Rochelle, and since my window overlooked the field we were in, we stepped through my door mere moments after finishing the little talk that thankfully hadn't led to my arrest after all.

He moved from one foot to the other as he gazed about my home. Then he realized what he was doing and stopped. Stood a bit straighter if that was possible. Realized what he was seeing and frowned his puzzlement. "Two rooms. Two. I expected one. Maybe it is adequate after all." He looked around again, at the plants all over the place. "Why all the flowers?"

"They aren't flowers, they are cuttings from the apple orchard and a few other places nearby."

"Aren't there enough plants outside?" The frown deepened, and he shuddered slightly. "The whole ship is filled with green things and you want more?"

"I'm a botanist." I was glad for the time spent inserting my credentials into the Destiny's database. It was all there, the schools, the degrees, and the experience. Of course, the experience was in family-owned businesses but that fact was glossed over so anyone looking would only know that I'd done numerous internships for prestigious companies. No one had to know that I'd been involved in the business of growing things ever since I was old enough to walk. "I like plants. I like to grow them. I like experimenting with them." Cullen Vail clearly did not have a green thumb, which was good because most of the plants in the apartment were experimental in nature. Just in case I'd need them later when things went bad.

"Why don't you do your experiments in the greenhouses with the other botanists?"

It was my turn to step from one foot to the other. My turn to stop doing so before he figured it meant I was uncomfortable with his question. "I didn't sign on as a botanist, rather as a farmer." At his expression, I quickly added, "And I love it. I love being a farmer. But I like to mess around a bit on my own time." I waved to the pots of green things on every available surface. "As you can see."

His body language was exquisite. Eyebrows raised, body hunched for protection from killer plants, nostrils flared because what he truly wanted was out of there and he planned on going as soon as he could figure out a way. "Okay." He licked his lips. "If you're sure the apartment is okay ..."

"Do you want to see the bedroom?"

"No, no, that won't be necessary." He backed a step towards the still-open door. "I can see that I had the wrong idea about the smaller apartments. They are quite adequate after all. Much larger than ... " But he never said what was smaller than my apartment. He just kept backing until he was in the hallway, where he turned smartly, closed the door, and disappeared.

I sagged onto the couch and didn't move for the better part of an hour. Then I paced back and forth. I couldn't stop. I knew it was nerves and that there was no place to go to for comfort, no one to talk to. Unless ...

There was someone after all. Wilkes Zander, the town Mayor and everyone's grandfather. I couldn't tell him why I was upset but I wouldn't have to. He knew already. We'd talk around it because we had an unwritten pact never to admit to each other that I was a stowaway, but he would understand, and I needed someone to understand.

I went in search of a faux grandfather, my thinking changed one hundred and eighty degrees from what it had been earlier. Before Cullen Vail. Now all I could think about was how life on the Destiny was one gigantic lie after another. Fake dirt, fake sky, fake credentials and fake grandfather. But I was the biggest lie of all.

I found Wilkes seated on a bench in the town square. Right beside Cullen Vail. The two were deep in conversation so I turned to leave until Wilkes Zander called out to me. "Hey, Elle. Come join us. We were just talking about you."

I'd have to get used to my throat closing up every time someone said something that could remotely be interpreted as knowing what and who I was. Maybe relaxation techniques would help. Maybe. In the meantime, though, I must join them or raise suspicion. "I'm kind of busy. Later?"

Wilkes waved my protests aside and patted the seat beside him. I didn't dare object and he'd be between Cullen Vail and myself, so I sat. "Cullen says you're a botanist." I nodded mutely. "You are wasted as a farmer. You should be working in the greenhouses." I opened my mouth to say something but he shushed me with a look. "I know you're a great farmer, a wonderful farmer." At my surprised look, he smiled. "You think I don't know what goes on around here but I do. I know that you bring in more produce than anyone else in the area. Possibly more than anyone else on the Destiny."

"I try." I licked my lips. Had I forgotten the cardinal rule in my family and outshone someone else? I should know better. I did know better. I knew to never call attention to myself. But I'd tried so hard to fit in that I'd done the opposite. I'd called attention to myself big time. "The apple trees deserve all of the credit."

"It's more than that, Elle, and you know it. You're talented. You do something that most of us don't. Something different, I think. Something that only a botanist would know to do. I'm thinking it's something that should be noticed by those idiots in charge." He pulled back and examined me closely. There was just a hint of puzzlement in that look, as if he knew there was more to my story than being a stowaway, but he didn't know what it was and he wouldn't ask. Yet. "Cullen and I have been talking about moving you to the greenhouses with the other specialists, where your talents can be put to good use."

"I told you that I don't want … "

He shushed me again. "It's not about what you want, Elle. It's about what's best for the Destiny. Seems there's some concern about the plants not producing as well as expected." He shook his head. "It's not a real concern, of course. Nothing they can't deal with. Why we have the best minds from Earth right there in the greenhouses and they are working on the problem. If it is a problem, if it's more than just a temporary glitch. But another mind looking at things won't hurt."

He stood up and I realized that part of the reason Cullen Vail had been so graceful earlier was the low gravity. Even elderly people like Wilkes moved with ease. "Anyway, now that you're here, you and Cullen can talk about it. I'm not needed for this particular conversation so I think I'll just mosey over to the café and see what their special is today."

Without Wilkes as a buffer, the space between us

wasn't nearly enough. I wanted to run away, to look elsewhere, to stop breathing if that would change what was happening, but I couldn't do any of those things. I stretched my lips in a parody of a smile and asked Mr. Vail what he was thinking.

"Cullen. Call me Cullen. No 'Mister'."

Cullen. "I'd rather harvest apples and cherries than work in the greenhouses."

"Let me take you to meet the scientists so you can see what they are doing." I opened my mouth but he continued before I could speak. "And you might like to see the animal barns too. I've noticed that farmers find that kind of thing interesting."

I reminded him that I was a botanist, not a farmer, and then, as that small smile I'd already recognized as belonging to Cullen Vail and no one else ghosted across his face, I realized I'd fallen neatly into his trap and was stuck. I wasn't a farmer and I'd admitted it. I was a botanist and, as such, I was going to the greenhouses with Cullen Vail.

No, not Cullen Vail, just Cullen. The head of Security wanted me to call him by his first name. Was that ironic or what?

I expected we'd take the elevator back to the tube that ran along the center of the Destiny and ride that to the greenhouses but instead I was led to the town square and a little beyond, to a narrow road I'd seen but not paid any attention to because I never went anywhere. We climbed onto what looked like a Harley with an electric motor. It had Security written on one side. I wrapped my hands around the iron that was

Cullen's waist and leaned into his back as we started off towards the center of the Destiny. The heart of the beast. To the hub of government, commerce, science and just about everything else necessary for people to live together in harmony. Except, of course, for the Captain's bridge. That reigned in lofty superiority at the end of that central tube. At the front of the ship.

I expected the hub to be a city and when Cullen parked his bike, I realized that I was right. And wrong. Buildings there ringed the Destiny like a belt around its middle, scattered in a haphazard arrangement of no particular design, though I knew they followed a plan. I just didn't know what it was. "Welcome to Center City."

"Not a very imaginative name."

"It's the center of government and it's in the center of the Destiny."

Cullen led the way to the greenhouses. They weren't far from the parking lot, just past a few buildings devoted to animal husbandry and a couple more that were fisheries. I followed, wishing I was somewhere else. Anywhere else because I've been in the horticulture business all my life and I knew what was waiting for me, even if Cullen didn't.

If I'd applied for a berth on the Destiny as a botanist I'd not have been chosen even though I was a double honors student with extensive credentials and a couple semi-major discoveries to my name and I knew large numbers of important people in the field. Because those things, impressive as they were, wouldn't have been enough to get me accepted. Only political pull would have done that and those who'd used their influential friends to get them on board would resent me big time.

When we stepped into the closest greenhouse my heart sank. This was going to be bad. The scientists were polite enough to Cullen but it was soon clear to both of us that they didn't like him pushing me onto them any more than they liked having me around. They threw mental darts at us both.

I knew that as soon as Cullen left, if I stayed they'd tear me limb from limb. I didn't want to think what would happen if they discovered my secret. And they probably would because professionals who have had an outsider thrust into their midst will stop at nothing to destroy the interloper. Me.

Cullen was good at his job. He read their thoughts exactly and their intentions. Being the kind of man he was, I knew he'd feel responsible if anything happened. Even if nothing happened he'd feel guilty for bringing me there and subjecting me to their criticism. I knew he'd want to do something to remedy things. And he did.

First, he looked around in a seemingly aimless way that took in everything, then he stepped closer to me and slipped one arm around my waist, a seemingly casual gesture but no one was fooled. I was under his protection and no one had better mess with me. His gesture would keep them well behaved while he was there. After he left would be a different matter.

"Mind if we take a look around?" he asked mildly. The head grower blinked and then nodded reluctantly.

He couldn't very well start an argument with the head of Security, which meant Cullen was higher up in the pecking order of the Destiny. So all he did was make a half turn to indicate where we should start our tour. Cullen's arm around my waist tightened as he moved us in the direction the grower had pointed. The heart of the greenhouses.

As we neared the first table in the first greenhouse, I felt something. A wrongness. An itch at the back of my neck. Everything looked fine to the untrained eye, but my eye was trained and had been honed over a lifetime of watching things grow. Of helping them grow. Of fixing problems when they didn't grow right. So I knew that the plants in that greenhouse were in trouble and that trouble was worse than Wilkes Zander had intimated.

I felt their pain in my gut but any experienced botanist even those without my extra senses could see the slight droop to the leaves and the thinness of the stems. There was also a lack of health in the roots that I couldn't see but could sense. The scientists in the other room knew I saw it because they saw it. And they didn't like the fact that I knew they had a problem.

The head grower had followed us. I turned, still wrapped in Cullen's arm, and gave him a questioning look. He shrugged. "A small problem. Nothing we can't handle." He dared me to argue further.

"I'm sure you'll fix things." I subsided and let Cullen sweep me away from the grower and the others still standing where we'd left them. We went to the other side of the main room, into a second greenhouse. I cried privately for the plants that were struggling in this alien environment but there was nothing I could do. Not now. My only influence at the moment was with the apple orchard and the cherry bushes. They were fine and once I was back home in New Rochelle I'd try to figure out a way to help the poor plants in the greenhouses without appearing to do so. Because the botanists who worked there would tear me limb from limb if I did anything noticeable.

The head grower left us alone as Cullen half-dragged me between the rows of tables to still a third greenhouse filled with tomato plants. There were acres of them, all red and ripe but with something subtly wrong, something I could see and the other botanists could see but Cullen was clueless about. He stopped. "Sorry about their stupidity, Elle."

He turned me until I stood before him. We were inches apart. He'd probably not been this close to another human being for years, at least not willingly. A whiff of his uniform, the soap he used to wash it, the leather belt and the metal buttons washed over me. And something else. Cullen Vail himself.

He clearly hadn't expected us to be so close when he brought me around and it rendered him speechless for a moment. He took a step backwards and bumped into a table filled with growing tomatoes. They'd been watered recently, they were wet, and droplets cascaded over him, spotting his immaculate uniform, beading on his perfect hair, pearling his skin. Not knowing what else to do, we both stared at the drops until they soaked into his uniform or evaporated. It took a while.

"I didn't know they'd react so badly." He scowled at the wet spots on his uniform as if staring would scare them into drying faster. "They shouldn't do that. They are professionals."

"That's the problem."

He slumped as he realized what I'd said. "I brought someone into their domain and they feel threatened."

"Yes."

He sighed, a sound pulled from his toes. "Every time I try to do something right, it backfires." Then he realized he'd spoken out loud and stiffened. Turned into a statue. Became overly competent.

When had he tried to do something right and failed? What had the consequences been? I pretended not to notice. "I like being a farmer. I'm happy where I am." I touched his face. I shouldn't have done so but he was so unhappy that I couldn't help myself.

He bent closer and studied me for a moment, taking my hand that was touching his face into his own for a second before letting it drop. Then he shook his head as if clearing out cobwebs. "I'll take you home to New Rochelle." His demeanor changed. The trip was finished except for the return. The stormy eyes changed again, not banked fire this time but something different. I couldn't imagine what it was. "But I don't like the way they treated you. No one acts like that on my watch. On the way out let's give them something to think about."

His arm wrapped itself tightly around my waist as

we retraced our steps. We were so close that anyone watching would think we were lovers. The greenhouse workers would think tha and they'd know they'd come close to hexing the head of Security's girlfriend.

We said a pleasant goodbye to their glowering faces and exited the greenhouse, still with our arms wrapped around each other. That lasted until we turned a corner. We separated hastily. Cullen might have shivered in relief but the motion was so slight I couldn't be sure.

As we climbed onto his bike, he asked, "What was all that stuff you professionals were talking about back there? Everything looked fine to me. Was Wilkes right? Is there a problem?"

"The plants aren't as healthy as they should be."

"Is it serious?" He was ready to start the bike but didn't. Instead he straddled it and gave me all of his attention. "Tell the truth, Elle. It's important. Crucial. The plants keep us alive. They provide not only food but oxygen. If there's something seriously wrong, I need to know."

"I promise nothing will go wrong." I should have let it go at that. Got on the bike and waited for him to start it. But I didn't. "Why? What could you do if there is a problem? Your sphere is security, not plants."

"What I do with all problems beyond the scope of my job. Tell the Captain. After that what happens would be his call."

"Would he turn the Destiny around and return to earth?"

"We've passed the point of no return."

His words hit me with the force of a freight train. The point of no return. If I was caught, I'd not be sent home. So what would happen? How bad would it be? I shivered. Seeing my trembling, Cullen reached towards me. Stopped. Didn't know the proper procedure for this situation. Decided to wing it and wrapped me in his arms and pulled me close, though his body was still as stiff and proper as ever.

I collapsed into his strength, thinking as I did so how ironic it was that the man who could order me out an airlock was trying to comfort me. If I was discovered would he do the same before the airlock opened? Would he remember this moment and the way our bodies melded together so nicely? Would he regret that his job included such an awful thing as throwing me away like yesterday's garbage? Or would he do it without a second thought? "I'm sure the professionals will deal with the problem before it becomes serious enough to alert the Captain."

"I certainly hope so."

He unwound himself from me and started the bike and neither of us said anything during the trip home. I was so glad to be back in New Rochelle that I was tempted to fall down and kiss the ground. I would have if Cullen wasn't watching. I did after he left and I didn't feel foolish about it at all, even though it was fake dirt covering phony ground. It was my fake dirt and my phony ground. It belonged to me and everyone else on the Destiny. It was the foundation of our world, my world now, and I'd protect it with everything in me, no matter that it was phony. I promised that fake dirt that

I'd figure out what was wrong with the plants in the greenhouses and I'd fix it.

As I pushed open the door to my apartment, I thought back to what was happening in the greenhouses. I hadn't wanted to go there, but now I was glad I had because I knew that my family's fears were right. Things were going wrong and much sooner than any of us would have thought.

It was a good thing I'd succeeded in stowing away. Because in the coming weeks, possibly months, until I got things back on track, I would be all that kept ten thousand people alive.

Chapter Six

Alicia visited the next morning. Nothing new, she stopped by often to visit Braveheart. Sometimes she brought her own cat so mother and kitten could be together. During her visits she'd developed an interest in the potted plants all over my place. She liked the cherry blossoms best because of their delicate pink color. I'd promised to give her a tiny tree for herself and she was there to get it.

"You have to do what I taught if you want it to be healthy."

She held it tightly. "I promise."

"If it starts to droop, bring it back and I'll tell it to stand up straight." I laughed because it was a joke.

She liked jokes and giggled. Then she scared me. "Just like you tell the orchard to grow nice apples and cherries and they do."

She hadn't forgotten. I'd hoped she would. "I can't really do that. I was being silly. Sometimes I talk to myself."

"Like Grandpa Zander?"

"Yep. Just like him."

She giggled again. She was enjoying this conversation. "No one pays attention to Gramps when he talks to himself but when you talk to the orchard, it listens. Trees like you." She held out the miniature cherry tree I'd potted for her, not caring that I could talk to trees because in her child's world it wasn't important. "It's pretty. Will it grow big?"

"Not if you keep it in the pot. It'll stay the right size for the pot."

I stared out my window long after she left, shaking like a rag. I liked Alicia but there were times I wished we'd never met. It was because of her that I had an apartment and was an accepted resident of New Rochelle, not to mention that I had a kitten. But if she blurted out what she knew to the wrong people, I could end up in jail.

I shook my head. What was I thinking? She was a child. Who pays attention to children? Who believes them? I should stop worrying and get outside and be sociable. I should go for a walk. Everyone walked everywhere in New Rochelle, it was great exercise and a good way to find out what was happening in town because gossips also took walks.

I headed towards the town square because that's where I was most likely to find people, but no one I knew was there. On the other side of the square, however, several people were clustered around the harvesting center building. I knew them from delivering apples and cherries so I sauntered over. Gerald, the guy who checked deliveries, wasn't busy. No one was, which was unusual. Most days the harvest center was a bustling place. "Elle." He waved a couple of fingers in my direction. "What's doing? No apples today?"

There could be. Trees in the orchard were heavy with fruit but I didn't dare bring too much too often. "Not yet. Soon." I looked around. "Slow day?"

There was no humor in his laugh. "Slow week. Several slow weeks."

"How so?" The hairs on the back of my neck rose. Was it beginning?

"Not as good a harvest lately as we'd like." Gerald put on a positive face. It was hard but he managed. "But it'll pick up."

One of the guys agreed. "Yeah, it'll get better. Elle's apples and cherries are growing great. So maybe some of the other crops are slow, they'll catch up and it'll get back to what it should be. You'll see."

Another spoke slowly and without the positive lilt of the first speakers. "If that doesn't happen, I'm going to ask Elle to visit my blueberries and wave her magic wand or do whatever she does to make her crops the best on the Destiny."

They all laughed, and someone said something about witches, and then ducked, laughing harder, as I stuck out my tongue at him.

It was a good visit until Gerald ruined the mood. "Cullen Vail was here a bit ago, asking about you."

"Me?" A headache started pounding the back of my neck. "What did he want?"

Gerald leered. "I think he likes you."

"Not a chance." I relaxed slightly.

Gerald looked me up and down. "Who'd have thought our illustrious, slightly pompous head of

Security would fall for a lowly farmer?"

Someone else broke in. "He didn't fall for a farmer. Remember what he said? Our Elle isn't just any farmer. She's got degrees. She's special. She knows more about growing food than all of us lowly dirt farmers put together."

The man with the blueberries spoke again. "Now I know I'm going to ask Elle to check out my berries. No wonder she brings in the best crops. She's an expert."

I puffed out my cheeks to hide my discomfort. "He had no right to tell you that."

Gerald waved a charitable hand. "Don't worry, Elle. We promise not to hold all those degrees against you as long as you continue to bring in great crops and teach us your secrets." He leaned against the wall and crossed one leg over the other. "You see, Elle, there's a little competition going on that you might not know about. But you're a part of it, like it or not. New Rochelle isn't the best producer on the Destiny yet but, with you around, it might be very soon. The other villages aren't bringing in crops like they did, and we are getting better thanks to your cherries and apples. As soon as you teach us what you know, New Rochelle will be on the map and everyone else can eat our dust."

There were a few 'hear, hears' and then everyone decided it was time to return to what little work there was for them. I wandered away, comforted by the knowledge that at least one small group of people on the Destiny wanted me. As I rounded the corner of the building, I wondered what they'd say if they knew the truth about me. The real truth.

My attention was caught by an individual in a uniform talking to someone. Cullen Vail was in town and he was asking questions about me. It hadn't been two weeks since his last visit. He wasn't on schedule, so why was he here? The headache turned into a pounding, scary pain through my whole body.

I hid behind the building while I debated whether to continue towards the grocery store to pick up some sweet peppers or head back to my apartment and hide. But when I peeked around the corner again he was gone so I cautiously headed down the single street that was the village of New Rochelle towards the village square.

I decided he must be headed for his Harley to run some official errand or other. He'd most likely stopped in New Rochelle because it was on his way to somewhere else and that was how he'd ended up talking to the farmers. No other reason. He hadn't come because of me. About me. I was safe, the hurting began to subside.

A middle-aged lady in the grocery store stopped me in the cereal aisle. "Cullen Vail was here."

"Oh?" I pretended surprise.

"He asked about you."

"Me?" My voice squeaked. This wasn't good. Maybe he wasn't just passing through. But it wasn't necessarily bad either. I frantically told myself that there were a thousand reasons for him being in town that had nothing to do with me. But I couldn't dismiss the fact that he'd asked about me. "Was he looking for me?'

"No. He was just curious." She grabbed a box of cereal. "He tried to hide it, though." She gave me the once-over slyly. "Didn't work. I can tell when a man is interested in someone. The questions he asked were ... well ... personal."

"I don't think ... "

"Dear, don't even try to deny it. It seems that our Cullen Vail is human after all."

"I doubt ... "

"I always thought of him as being too standoffish to ever have a real relationship. But it looks like I was wrong." She shuddered delicately and turned up a snub nose. "And, Elle, don't take this the wrong way, but you're welcome to him. He's way too stiff for most of us."

"What exactly did he ask?" I made myself go still.

"Oh, whether I like you or not. Whether you fit in with the other residents of New Rochelle, which of course you do. Things like that, until Wilkes Zander came along and let him know that he didn't appreciate anyone of any status whatsoever, even an important Security person, asking questions of a personal nature about our people. He suggested that if Cullen wanted to know anything about you he should ask you himself."

"I hope ... "

"Don't be surprised if he shows up at your doorstep."

I hope not. But I smiled and stepped around her on my way to the sweet peppers. Which weren't as large as usual. Another sign something was wrong?

When I returned home I approached my apartment cautiously. If Cullen was there, I'd disappear and wait until he was gone. But he wasn't so I went inside and locked the door.

Restless, I stared out my window. What I saw gave me pause. Cullen Vail was in the field and he was talking with Alicia. Sweet, gossipy Alicia who knew most, if not all, of my secrets. She had her cat in her arms, as usual. She held it out to Cullen who took it and held it away from him as if it might bite. But he managed not to drop it and petted it awkwardly twice before returning it to Alicia.

She said something and they both looked towards my apartment. My window. I ducked out of sight but still watched through the curtains. Alicia cuddled her cat and Cullen seemed interested in it. Was she telling him that I'd taken one of the kittens? Was it as simple as that? Nothing illegal about adopting a kitten so I relaxed. A little.

The two parted. Cullen strode towards the road and his Harley but Alicia remained with her cat. I opened my window. "Hey, Alicia." She looked up. "Want a cookie?" Fortunately I'd been baking and she liked sweets.

She gathered her cat and came to my apartment. I had the door open when she arrived and soon mother cat and kitten were playing happily while Alicia made quick work of a plate of cookies as she answered questions that I hoped didn't arouse her suspicions. But she didn't appear suspicious.

"You talked with Cullen Vail."

"Yep. He likes cats even though he couldn't take one of the kittens. But that's okay because you took the last one."

"He can play with your cat."

"That's what he said. He said he might come back to play with Queen another time."

"Did he say when?"

"Soon."

"What do you talk about when he visits?"

"Mostly he asks a lot of questions."

"Such as?"

"All kinds of things. Today he asked about you."

"Me?" I pretended to be surprised as I fought a growing unease. Cullen suspected something. Or not. I remembered that woman's assessment of him being good at his job. How good? "He didn't have to ask you. I could have told him anything he wants to know."

"He said he didn't want to bother you."

"What did he ask?"

"If you like your kitten. If I help you grow stuff in your apartment."

"What did you say?"

"I told him that you gave me a tiny tree. It's pretty."

"Was that all he asked?"

"There was more but I can't remember."

Normal questions. Perhaps he was interested in me as a woman after all and wasn't planning on arresting me, though somehow I couldn't picture him in a romantic relationship and not in any kind of relationship at all with me. But I relaxed somewhat. I'd been on the Destiny for months and nothing had happened. Except that I could never relax. I should remind myself of that every day. Every single day.

On the other hand, perhaps he just couldn't figure out why I wanted to be a farmer instead of a scientist which was a totally normal question. How many people spend as many years in school as I did and throw it all away to go out and grow cherries? Why ever he was asking about me, there was nothing I could do about it and no way to know the truth. So I tried to forget his visit to New Rochelle.

A few days later, I was in the apple orchard filling the cart with my weekly harvest of apples and cherries when I sensed someone behind me. I turned and saw Cullen framed by green branches and white blossoms. I caught my lower lip between my teeth as our glances met and held. He was out of uniform. I'd never seen him in anything other than the navy blue that the crew wore when on duty. He looked different. Human. Vulnerable.

He stepped forward. "Hello." Stopped and waited for me to acknowledge his presence. I inclined my head. "I was told I'd find you here. You are a creature of habit and today is your day to harvest fruit."

"As are you. A creature of habit. You come to New Rochelle every two weeks." I checked my comunit. "You're off schedule. So why are you here today?"

"I'm off duty."

"Of course. No uniform." But he didn't need one to tell the world that he was a guy in charge. His bearing was so straight and his movements so precise that his very self shouted that he was watching over everyone. Except I didn't want him to watch over me. I wanted him gone but I shouldn't say so.

He stepped closer, arms stiff at his side, and looked around. "I've been checking out what you said the other day. Now that you called my attention to it, I can see that not all crops are as healthy as these trees."

"So that's what you were about?"

"What do you mean?"

"Asking questions about me." He stopped walking. Stayed a safe distance away. Made a quarter turn away. Pretended to be relaxed but I knew better. "I heard all about your little visits with people who know me."

"That's my business. It's what I do."

"You didn't ask questions about other people. Not from what I heard. Just me." A good offence is the best defense, as my cousin Todd used to say. I hoped he was right as I plowed ahead in an effort to get Cullen out of my orchard and my life. "In future, if you want to know something about me, ask me, not someone else."

"I'll do that." My attack worked. He closed into himself and left with his back as ramrod straight as when he arrived. But as he ducked around the apples hanging heavy on the trees he said, "This fruit is wonderful. You're good." The words were hard to say, he sounded like he was choking on them. But Cullen Vail, the perfect security person would be honest if it killed him. "Those idiots in the greenhouses are making a mistake in ignoring you."

"They made their choice." The trees closed behind him, shooing him along and closing ranks behind him so I found myself yelling impotently at leaves still quivering from his passing instead of at Cullen himself. I'd have liked to see his expression but the fact that I could only imagine what he looked like didn't keep me from smiling as I followed his soft curses through the trees. The orchard was a good friend and was acting accordingly.

Could it be that his questions hadn't been personal in nature? That his only concern was failing crops and my potential to turn things around?

I left the orchard as soon as I figured Cullen was good and gone. I went home and found Alicia at my door, her cat at her feet and her miniature cherry tree in her hands. It was drooping. "What's with this?" I took it from her after unlocking the door and leading her and Queenie inside.

"It's sad. I think it misses the other trees."

"It was nice of you to bring it for a visit." I set it on a small table already laden with other growing things and I touched it gently. In moments it perked up. "See, it's better now and I'm pretty sure that it'll be okay. I doubt you'll have to bring it for another visit." I touched it again, just to be sure, as Alicia's lower lip stuck out. "But, of course, you can bring it over any time you wish." The lip receded somewhat. "Do you have time for cookies?"

A huge sigh shook her frame. "Mom says I'm

eating too many cookies."

"Maybe one?"

She sat on the couch and nibbled a single cookie slowly so as to make it last as long as possible. While she nibbled, she crossed her ankles primly. "Mr. Vail asked about you."

"I know. You told me."

"I mean again. He came again."

Fear crawled through my stomach. I had to force myself not to double over. "When?"

"Just now. When I was on my way here. I showed him my tree. He said you might be able to help it. Then he asked questions."

I won't panic. I refuse to panic. "What kind of questions?"

"You know. Questions." And that was all I got. Her miniature cherry tree was so healthy it glowed, Queenie was getting restive and the cookie was long gone. "I have to go now." With a cat under one arm and a cherry tree under the other, she left and I was left alone to try and make my stomach settle down. I folded over and stayed that way for a long time.

Then I went to the window. Stared at the apple orchard and a group of kids playing baseball. The everyday scenes should have made me feel better but they didn't. Nothing could because Cullen Vail was on the edge of the field and he was talking with Alicia. I had no doubt I was the topic of conversation.

I closed the curtains and waited as I fought nausea and told myself that Cullen Vail wouldn't come. He wouldn't. He'd go back to wherever he came from and would forget all about me. Still, I folded my hands over my stomach and wished I was somewhere else. Anywhere else. Like back on Earth.

When the knock came it was almost a minute before my body could unknot enough to answer but I couldn't delay forever so eventually I swung it open. As I'd expected, Cullen Vail stood before me. Taller than I remembered, solemn of demeanor, almost grim, but polite. Oh so polite. "Miss Olmstead?"

"My name is Elle."

I gestured for him to come in but he stayed where he was, framed by the doorway, filling it, a perfectly formed man in a perfectly rectangular opening. Both man and opening were functional and impersonal.

"Miss Olmstead, it has come to my attention that your name wasn't on the Destiny's manifest at launch. Nor was it on any list of colonists. Nor did it appear anywhere at all until after we'd past the outer planets and were approaching the edge of the solar system."

"Really?" Would it help to pretend I didn't know what he was talking about? "I can't imagine why not."

"Miss Olmstead?" He folded his arms and waited.

I wilted. Died. Gave up right then and there. I'd tried but, like my cousins, I'd failed. I didn't have any tricks up my sleeve, no story that he'd believe, no way to prevent whatever he had planned. I wasn't cut out to be a felon, I didn't have the stomach for a life of crime. "I don't have any explanation."

He stepped inside, filling the apartment as he'd filled the doorway, competent and authoritarian. "Miss Olmstead, you are a stowaway. Accordingly, you are under arrest for the crime of boarding the Destiny illegally. I'll have to ask you to put your hands behind your back." I did so and felt binders tightening around them. "Now I'll ask you to come with me." He ushered me towards the door.

"What about Braveheart? My kitten? What'll happen to him?"

"I'll talk to Wilkes Zander. He'll think of something."

"Someone has to take care of Braveheart until this is straightened out."

"You mean *if* it's straightened out."

"It will be. It's a mistake, it's just a mistake."

"Then you'll be home shortly."

If I wasn't? Would Braveheart suffer the same fate that awaited me? I couldn't bear to think of both of us being tossed out of the airlock. He was a sweet kitten, he deserved better. What I'd done was deliberate but his only crime was being born. Barring a miracle, though, I'd not be back to save him and we'd both be treated like yesterday's trash.

Everyone in New Rochelle watched me being dragged ignominiously towards the elevator. Alicia was there, along with her mother and grandfather.

My eyes met those of Wilkes Zander. He didn't like what was happening but there was nothing he could do. I blinked to let him know that I'd not betray him. No one would ever know he'd willingly helped a stowaway.

I stopped beside Alicia, letting my body go so limp that Cullen had to drag me and stop. "Alicia." She came close, uncertain as to what was going on but knowing that whatever was happening wasn't good. "Braveheart is in my apartment. Take care of him, will you?"

"Okay." Her eyes were big. Then, for once in her life, she shut up.

"And the plants. Water them, will you?" She said she would and then I started walking again so Cullen didn't have to drag me away. By the time we reached the town square I was walking proudly, straight and as tall as anyone five two can walk and as far away from Cullen Vail as my restraints would allow. I was going to jail but I'd go with my head held high.

Chapter Seven

The ascent in the elevator was excruciating. Neither of us spoke, nor did we look at each other. I used the time to watch the ground fall away and the trees and bushes grow smaller as we rose towards the huge tube that was the center of the Destiny, wondering when, if ever, I'd see growing things again. Cullen had secured me to a pipe so he didn't have to touch me during our ride. As soon as he was sure I couldn't break free he went to the opposite side and stayed there.

As we rose, and gravity grew less, we began floating and I tried to grab a strap so as not to end up twisting and turning against my restraints. A slight sound caught my attention. I tried to see where it came from but when I moved my head my entire body followed, and I found myself somersaulting over and over as the restraints on my wrists grew tighter and threatened to cut off circulation.

I located the source of the sound but didn't look because I was busy trying to loosen my restraints. I soon discovered that I didn't have to look because the source came to me. Cullen Vail coming over. He grabbed my restraints, using them as a fulcrum and stopping my tumbling motion. He slid his comunit over them and they released enough for the circulation to return to my wrists. Then a hand reached out and hauled me to the floor. Once my feet were planted precariously, a second hand guided me to the nearest strap.

"You're not used to the elevators."

"Obviously."

"I suppose stowaways have reason to avoid the operations center." He didn't try to disguise the contempt in his voice. Then it hardened as he had a thought. "Unless it would be to plant a bomb." He whirled me around so hard that it hurt. I winced but this time he didn't care. "Is that why you're on the Destiny? To blow it up?" I couldn't stop whirling and would have grown dizzy had his hand not stopped me abruptly.

"How can you think such a thing?"

"I was there when the colonists said goodbye. I saw the crowds, the riots, and I read the signs. A lot of people would like to see the Destiny fail. They'd like to see the entire colonization program fail. A bomb would do that nicely."

"I'd die with everyone else."

"Some people don't care. Fanatics. Lunatics. Lots of people."

"That's not why I'm here."

"Why are you here?" He stuck his face in mine. We were inches apart. I'd never been that close to a man without it leading to a kiss but that was the last thing on his mind.

I took a deep breath as we stared at each other.

He'd never believe me, but with his face so close, his eyes so angry and his body so forbidding, I couldn't think up a convincing lie and I didn't want to. Didn't want to have to lie any more.

I was suddenly tired. All my life I'd been taught to keep what we did secret, and I'd done so but the doing had taken a toll. Staring into his angry eyes, I wanted to let it all come out. Not that the anger would dissipate but it would help to say it out loud. To speak for me, for my ancestors, for all of my family who'd worked so hard for so many years to save lives and been shunned for our trouble. Been hunted like witches. Been sent away.

So, right then and right there I made a decision and I told the truth, knowing it wouldn't be believed because it never is but needing to say it anyway. "I stowed away in order to save the crops that keep everyone alive."

Some of the fire left his eyes. He knew I was a botanist and that the crops were in trouble. He couldn't possibly know how bad it was going to get but that scant knowledge gave him momentary pause. He leaned back so he could see me from a safe distance though he didn't let go for fear I'd drift off. He bit his lips in thought.

I was emboldened. "I'm saving the crops because I can. Because I'm different. Because I'm not like you. I'm not like most people. I'm special. I'm very, very special."

He said the same thing that everyone would say if we told them about us. "I don't believe you."

"It's true. The crops are failing. Soon people won't have enough to eat. We knew it would happen … *I* knew it would happen … so I stowed away in order to be where I could fix things when everything went wrong."

He shook his head. "You're lying. You could have worked at the greenhouses but you refused. The *experimental* greenhouses. The place where changes would be made to save the crops. If they are, indeed, dying. If what you're saying is true, you'd have jumped at the chance to work there."

I despaired of him believing but I had to try. "You saw how I was treated. No one there would pay any attention to me or to anything I'd say. They'd never have done what was needed if for no other reason than that I suggested it."

"Or you preferred to work alone because it's hard to build a bomb with other people around. No one would notice in the middle of an apple orchard. You lived there for a while."

"I live in an apartment. I have friends. They visit. They'd see anything unusual."

"What about before? You could have done your dirty work before you got an apartment. Alicia said you lived in the orchard for a long time."

"I lived there because I'm a stowaway and didn't have any other place."

"Stowing away on a space ship is a felony."

"But that's all I'm guilty of and even that was because none of us were selected as crew or colonists. We tried but no one made the cut."

He blinked as what I was saying penetrated. "None of you? Are you saying you're not the only one?" Involuntarily he looked around as if to find more of my kind.

"I'm the only one on the Destiny."

"So you say."

"You don't have to search the ship. I'm the only one who made it on board though several of us tried." His eyes blazed and I knew that soon the ship would be searched inch by inch for both bombs and stowaways.

I tried again. "It's a long story." If he'd listen. I knew that even if he listened he wouldn't believe it. No one would. I closed my eyes in despair.

Through my eyelids I saw movement and I heard a harrumph, followed by, "Where you're going there'll be a lot of time to tell any story you can come up with. If I were you I'd make it a good one because the penalty for stowing away is severe."

I said nothing for the rest of the journey and neither did Cullen. When we reached the central tube and the elevator slowed and stopped he pulled me behind him as he floated towards a block of rooms beyond a door with a guard before it. As far as I could see along the tube, this was the only door that was guarded. Then I noticed the sign on the front. Law Enforcement. Cullen Vail's domain.

I was photographed, fingerprinted, swabbed for DNA, tied to a different, longer tether and read my rights, what few I had. As I floated about, careful not to get tangled in my prisoner restraints, I looked for the door to the prison but never found it. There were doors but they led to more and still more offices. When all was done, Cullen pointed me towards the entrance. Right back where we'd come from.

One of the officers asked, "Who do you want to escort her to jail?" So jail was somewhere else.

"I'll take care of it myself."

Work stopped. Mouths dropped open, but no one said a word. So quickly that I knew they were covering up their sudden work stoppage, they closed their mouths again and turned back to whatever they'd been doing while, without seeming to do so, they watched us. From behind paperwork, around screens, while swabbing spilled coffee from the air. Which meant Cullen Vail never escorted prisoners. Lesser officers handled such menial tasks. Until now.

Ignoring the silence and the electricity in the room, he shoved me towards the entrance. His aim was excellent, I would have sailed right through it if not for the tether connecting us. It was long enough that I wouldn't strangle myself and was made of a plastic-like substance that probably reacted in some way to the small device he held in one hand. I decided not to find out what it was or what would happen if I made a break for it.

He drew up to me and side by side we floated to the nearest elevator where I was shoved inside and tied like an animal to a pole. Again. The doors closed, and we started down. I was glad we were alone so there was no one to stare at me.

As gravity took hold, I slid down the pole until my feet were on the elevator floor and I found myself beside a window through which I could see the ground rushing up and the city that was the central hub of the Destiny. I recognized the greenhouses we'd visited earlier and the animal buildings. But from this height, I saw other buildings too. The courthouse. Beside it, connected by a tunnel, I saw the jail.

"Not large but it does the job."

"My new home."

"You should have thought of that when you stowed away."

"It had to be done. I told you why."

"You told a wildly imaginative tale that's not even close to credible. A child could have done better."

"It's the truth. You'll see. When the crops fail, when the plants die, when there isn't enough food."

His lips pressed together. "I don't think so." He looked away but before he was completely turned I saw pain. Or uncertainty, I wasn't sure which.

When the elevator reached the ground, we exited, and I was taken to jail. Paraded was more like it, for the area was crowded and everyone wanted to know what had happened and who I was and what I'd done. But Cullen ignored all questions and pushed me through the crowd and into the relative quiet of the courthouse rotunda. Then we went through one of the many doors, all guarded by officers in uniforms similar to Cullen's, and we were in the jail.

It was small but sufficient. Two of the half dozen cells were occupied and a bored deputy was at a desk. He looked up when we entered. "So this is the new prisoner. I was told she was coming. I've been waiting."

Cullen disconnected my tether, the deputy led me to one of the cells and shoved me inside. The door slid shut.

Cullen inspected the two other prisoners. "Jake again?"

"Drunk and disorderly. He'll be out in time for dinner."

"Who's the new guy?"

"Name's Byron. Got in a fight and broke someone's nose. He claimed self-defense but that'll be up to the court to decide."

"He's going to trial for a broken nose?"

"He insisted. Says it's his right. Wants a judge, jury, the works." The deputy looked over my information. "What about the woman? Will she go to trial?"

"That'll be up to the Captain. It's his jurisdiction. She's a stowaway so what happens is his call but I'm guessing he won't bother with a trial."

The deputy came close and gave me a once-over. "She's pretty, if there's a trial an all-male jury would set her free." He glanced at the instructions Cullen had put into the system. "This doesn't mention visitors. What do I do? We've never had a felon before."

"Of course she can have visitors. She has rights." He started away and then turned back, talking to the deputy, studiously avoiding me. "But if someone wants to see her, call me." He was thinking of my comment that there were others like me. If there were any of them on the Destiny, would they contact me?

"Should I make them wait until you get here?"

He thought, then shook his head. "Don't do that.

But do make sure the security cameras are rolling. And call me." Then he was gone and the deputy, after asking if I'd had lunch, disappeared to find me a meal and I was left alone at last to look around the small room that was now my home.

The jail ran on a schedule and I soon learned to judge time by what was happening instead of by checking my comunit. Lunch meant it was noon. Lights out was at ten. No one wanted to disturb Jake when he was sleeping it off so mornings were somewhat erratic. When he wasn't in jail, breakfast came early and began a gossipy time of day. When he was in the cell next to mine, which someone jokingly said was reserved for him, breakfast was hot cereal that I ate as quietly as possible so as not to wake him and the deputies tip-toed around while doing their chores. No one wanted to deal with Jake if he was still suffering from a hangover. Let him sleep long enough and he became reasonably decent.

The days passed. The prisoners who were there when I came were released and more were added. In time they, too, left and still more days passed, turning into weeks. The cells on either side could have had revolving doors for all the times prisoners came and went. But I remained.

The hours were long and boring both for inmates and guards so everyone ended up being my friend. I'm easy to be with and a good conversationalist and for the most part the other prisoners were regulars who I got to know quite well, though they came and went while I stayed.

I became pretty good friends with the guards too. They were nice guys who felt sorry for me. They didn't see how stowing away compared to the crimes of the other prisoners. They tried to make me comfortable. I got a new bed and bedding, better than the other prisoners had and they said Cullen Vail had approved the extra expense though privately I thought they said so to make me feel better. There was a belief in the entire Security contingent that there had been something between Cullen and me up to the time he arrested me and nothing I said could change their minds.

They also thought Cullen should have managed not to find me when he learned I was a stowaway. Or that he could have let me go. I heard them muttering among themselves and, finally, they said it out loud where I could hear and after that we got really chummy.

I never told them the story I'd told Cullen, the truth, though I was pretty sure they'd heard it because once the night deputy did suggest that I might have been left alone if I'd been able to think of a more normal reason for being on the Destiny. After all I had papers and a comunit and that would have been proof enough for most people and perhaps Cullen would have let it go if I'd been less creative.

They said many times that they wished Cullen hadn't dug into the manifest for my name. But whenever they said that, they rolled their eyes and we all laughed because of course Cullen would do whatever was necessary to do his job perfectly.

Most of the time they approved of that quality in their boss because it made their jobs easier. He was very efficient, they said. They just didn't see why he had to be quite so efficient in my case but once I was arrested there was nothing anyone in Security could do because the Captain had authority over stowaways and they were only holding me until he got around to hearing my case.

Which would be a long time, they said, because more pressing problems had his attention. Like dying plants. Failing crops. A shortage of food in the near future, followed by starvation and the inevitable anger and riots that would follow. I was in cold storage so I was put on a back burner and languished in jail, gossiped with the deputies and generally was bored silly.

Chapter Eight

One morning I was dozing between Jake who was sleeping it off in the cell to my left and someone new on my right, a teenager who decided to go jogging without bothering to dress first. She almost caused a riot and at the moment was too busy sulking to talk but the thought of another female nearby was nice. The deputies were busy so with no social event happening I was napping. Until the door opened and someone entered the jail and looked around. Two someones.

I opened one eye a crack and sat up fast. Alicia and her grandfather, Wilkes Zander, mayor of New Rochelle, stood in the middle of the main room. Alicia tenderly held a wilted plant. Braveheart was cradled in Wilkes' arms. He cleared his throat loudly until someone noticed and then he said, "We're here to visit Elle Olmstead."

"Ellle?" The deputy sat up, almost in shock. "No one visits Elle. At least no one ever has."

Wilkes looked over his shoulder towards me. "Sorry we didn't come sooner, Elle. Things have been going on."

"I know. Word gets around, even here. Especially

here. A food shortage?"

His sigh was answer enough. "But we're here now."

"Did Alicia have anything to do with your coming?" Her insistent tugs on his arm told me who was behind the visit.

"Yep." No one could hold out against the pint-sized politician-in-training for long. Wilkes pointed to the cherry tree in her hands. "It's almost dead, like most of the trees. She thinks you can bring it back to life."

"Maybe." Alicia loved that tree so she'd done everything she could. It wouldn't be as far gone as many of the plants on the Destiny.

"And I brought Braveheart for a visit. He misses you."

I came to the door of my cell and reached for my kitten. "I was worried about him."

Wilkes knew what I was saying without using words because we didn't want to talk about my possible demise in front of Alicia. "Don't worry about Braveheart. We're keeping him for now, but if you can't care for him later, Gerald will take him."

"Gerald?" The guy who tallied produce at the harvest center. I always took Braveheart and Gerald always petted him.

A frown appeared on Wilkes' brow. "Funny thing, that. When I asked Gerald to take Braveheart, somehow the conversation got around to you. He said the harvest from that particular orchard dropped precipitously as soon as someone else took over." He watched me closely but I didn't give away what I was thinking so he went back to the reason for the visit, turning imperiously to the deputy. "Well? Can we see Elle or not?"

The deputy quickly unlocked the cell door and Alicia entered but Wilkes remained outside, coming just close enough to hand Braveheart to me. My kitten mewed and jumped into my arms and snuggled against me, making me realized how much I'd missed his tiny body next to mine. "I have a meeting, Elle. That's why we came to the government center. An important meeting, so I have to go but I'll be back as soon as it's done. You know what it's about."

"Dying crops."

"Yep." His shoulders were slumped. It would be a difficult meeting.

The cell door shut on Alicia, Braveheart and myself. Wilkes left, leaving the deputy undecided about his next move. Cullen wanted to be informed of any visitors. He'd have to go into another room to make contact and he wasn't sure if he should leave me alone with Alicia. Until Alicia set her miniature cherry tree on my cot and hugged me, blubbering loudly. "I missed you."

"I missed you too." We hugged for a long time.

"My mom doesn't give me cookies."

"That's too bad. I wish I had some but I can't bake in here."

"My tree is sick. You have to make it well." Her head lifted as the deputy decided I wasn't likely to slit anyone's throat. He went into the inner office to contact Cullen and popped out moments later to say he'd go look for some cookies. Alicia took time from insisting I fix her tree to tell him what kind. She's big on chocolate chips.

As soon as he disappeared, I gently pried her from my waist and picked up the cherry tree. "It doesn't look too bad."

"Oh, that's good. I was worried." I took the tiny tree and turned it around a few times and then closed my eyes and did my thing. It was easy, I'd been doing it ever since one time when I was a kid and had an argument with a prickly pear cactus. My whole family had erupted into laughter when the cactus won. Then they'd showed me how to win arguments with plants and ever since I've been pretty good at it, even the ones with thorns.

I was fairly confident and it turned out I was right. When I opened my eyes, the tree was already changing. The branches lifted, the leaves brightened, the whole thing took on new life. Alicia clapped her hands in delight. "I knew you'd do it. Grandpa Wilkes said you couldn't but I knew better because I watched you fix trees in the orchard."

I handed it to her. "It's okay now but you can bring it back if it gets sick again."

She examined the tree one way and another. "All the trees are sick. All of them. Everywhere. They are ugly. You should make them well too."

"I can't now. I have to stay here for a while."

"Don't wait too long because they are really, really sick."

The deputy returned with a bag of cookies that he shared with all of us prisoners and Alicia. He leaned back in his chair and ate about half the bag himself but it was a large bag, we were all satisfied, and Alicia said it was a nice party and Jake and the teenaged streaker agreed though she did comment that if she ate too many she might not have the same effect the next time she went for a stroll sans clothes.

When the cookies were finished, and Alicia had brushed the crumbs from her shirt, we talked quietly while I played with Braveheart. Then Wilkes returned. He collected his granddaughter, the cat and the tree and they prepared to leave.

Before that happened, Cullen burst into the room and looked wildly about. "She had visitors? Who? Where? Did you get their names?" He dashed to the deputy's desk and checked the visitor's roster. "Wilkes Zander and Alicia?" The deputy nodded and pointed. Then he stepped in front of them so they couldn't leave until Cullen stood face to face with Wilkes. "What are you doing here?"

"Visiting a friend. Elle is our friend."

Cullen's demeanor changed. Confronted by Wilkes' social grace, he remembered his manners. He shook Wilkes' hand and bent down to say something to Alicia but, seeing what was in her hands, he asked instead, "What's that?"

She held up the miniature cherry tree. "It's my tree. It was sick. Elle made it well."

Cullen's face thinned. "And how did she do that? Did she give it water?"

Alicia was indignant. "I water it everyday so it has enough water. She just fixed it. She made it well."

He took the tree and held it high. "How, exactly?"

"The way she made the apple trees well when they didn't feel so good."

"What apple trees?" He looked around for nonexistent trees. He was having a hard time dealing with Wilkes and Alicia. I understood, for they were a formidable pair.

"The ones in the orchard where she used to live. If they didn't feel good she fixed them. I watched her do it. I tried to do it myself but I guess I'm not old enough yet. So when my tree got sick, I brought it here. My grandpa didn't want to bring me but I was really, really nice so he did and he brought Braveheart too because Braveheart missed Elle almost as much as the trees miss her but trees can't walk so they couldn't come. Just my tree and Braveheart."

Cullen stood extremely straight and tried not to look confused as he turned the tree around and around in his hands. Then he looked daggers at me but, though I felt every invisible thrust, I refused to lower my gaze. We tried to stare each other down but it was a draw.

At long last, after one more puzzled look at the cherry tree, he returned it to Alici,a and she and her grandfather left. Then he stood lost in thought in the middle of the room until finally he turned to the deputy. "Did you notice the tree the little girl brought it?" The deputy nodded. "Was it the same tree she brought out?"

The deputy chewed his lower lip. "Now that you mention it the one she left with did seem different from the one she took into the cell."

"And you were here the whole time. She couldn't have sneaked a different one in?" The deputy's expression gave him away and he was forced to admit that he'd gone out for cookies. And he sheepishly mentioned that Wilkes Zander hadn't been locked in my cell.

"He brought a different tree. They hoodwinked you. You left them alone and they did their trick. It's part of a plot to give credence to that ridiculous story of hers but it won't work because we'll find the sick tree and prove them liars."

Almost instantly they were in my cell tearing apart everything that wasn't nailed down. But they found nothing. Cullen towered over me, his face a mask. "What did they bring and where did you hide it? Tell me!"

"She brought a tree and she took it with her. Same tree and I didn't hide anything."

"You're lying."

"Then where is it?" The cell was torn asunder, the prisoners on either side wide awake and watching. This was the most excitement since they'd been incarcerated.

"It was all recorded," the deputy said quietly because the prisoners on either side of me were more interested than they should be. "We can watch the recording."

"Of course." Cullen nodded shortly. "I'll do that.

Me, I'll watch and see what she did while you actually do your job and stick around so no one escapes." He turned without another word, stomped into the inner office and slammed the door. That was all we heard for possibly an hour. Then the door opened slowly, and he stepped out and came straight to my cell. "You." He pointed to me. "Come." The deputy opened my cell door and I followed Cullen into that private office.

A screen covered most of one wall. Cullen indicated that I sit, then he flipped a switch and soon I was watching my visit with Alicia. It started with her hug, then Braveheart being cuddled, and soon after I saw Alicia handing me the cherry tree. I saw me touching it until it came back to life.

He replayed the visit several times in total silence. Then he bent close enough for me to see that his eyes weren't solid black and that was close indeed because I saw clearly the pure night and lightning and thunder in them. They had dark flecks, too, and some not so dark and were night water and wind as well as lightning and thunder. They were beautiful and deep and frightening all at the same time. "Tell me what you did in there."

"I made the cherry tree well."

"What did you do and how did you do it? More importantly, what other magic tricks do you know that you might use on an unsuspecting victim?" He was so close I could see his nostrils flare and the tiny lines fanning out from his eyes.

"It wasn't a trick. I told you that I'm good with plants. I make things grow. It's what I do. It's why I'm here."

His eyes slitted and then he turned wordlessly and left, locking the door behind him. I shrank into my chair and stared at the ceiling, knowing at last how all those generations of relatives had felt those few times when they'd told people what we can do. About our abilities. And I waited, not knowing what would happen next but knowing that whatever it was it would probably be as terrible as it had been for all those previous generations.

He returned half an hour later carrying a half-dead tomato plant. I knew where he'd gotten it. From the greenhouse. Our eyes met briefly over the plant, remembering our time there, and then slid away as he stuck it towards me. "Prove it. Show me."

I examined it without touching it. "It's pretty sick."

"I knew it. You're a fraud."

"I didn't say that. I can probably make it better though I don't know if it'll ever be truly healthy again. Like I said, it's pretty sick but if you want me to, I'll try."

He shoved the pot towards me. "Do more than try. Fix it. Or else."

I touched the tomato plant gently. It had been handled roughly. Cullen didn't know about plants and he'd been angry when he chose it so it hurt and I felt its pain. But it wasn't dead so I tried. I closed my eyes and set my mind free.

It didn't take long. Moments later, I opened my eyes and smiled. "It wasn't as sick as I first thought. It'll be okay. Just give it a minute or two."

He waited, managing to stare holes through my body even as he stared at the tomato plant that responded faster than I'd thought. I don't know why I was surprised. Most things do respond quickly to decent care.

It stood straighter. Its leaves lifted towards the ceiling. It stretched to its full height and the first of many future blossoms unfurled along a vine. As each thing happened I felt it in the way that I always feel what's happening with plants. I couldn't help the smile that appeared and spread until it filled my whole being. I looked at Cullen and smiled even more because he was staring at the tomato plant as if waiting for it to bite him. He was shocked speechless.

I, on the other hand, felt pretty good. "I told you so."

He answered as if in a trance. "I don't know what you did, I don't know how you did it, but you weren't faking. I was careful. There's no other tomato plant to replace the sick one with. There's not a single healthy tomato plant on the Destiny so I know you couldn't trick me." He raked one hand through his hair, leaving it rumpled, the first time I'd seen him less than perfect. "I don't know how you do what you do, but I accept that you do it."

"I do." I waited because he wasn't finished.

"Did you know that the Destiny is already facing a crisis from a shortage of food?"

"I've heard talk."

"You can prevent it like you said?"

"I can."

You. Just you."

"Yes." I stood straight and tall and smiled until my

face was stiff. No matter what happened next, at that moment I was proud of myself and my family.

He snapped out of his reverie and stared at me accusingly. "You can save everyone yet you do nothing. You just sit here and do nothing."

I waved my hand to the room and towards the room holding the deputy, Jake and the streaker. "I'm in jail. It's hard enough to do what I do through the walls of a normal building but these walls are different. Worse. Impenetrable."

"Of course they are. It's a jail. Thin walls wouldn't hold a flea."

"If you want me to save the Destiny, you have to set me free."

"You stowed away."

"I did so to prevent what is already happening and right now I'm all that stands between life and death for ten thousand people."

He bit his lower lip. "I don't have the authority."

"Talk to the Captain."

"He's busy. He hasn't slept in days, maybe weeks."

"Because of the food shortage."

"I can't get near him. Hell, I can't even get close enough to call out his name. He has meetings all the time."

"If I stay in here, then very soon those meetings won't matter."

He licked his lips and then stood up and paced back and forth. Then he said, "Okay. I'll take you out myself."

"You'll break the law?"

He stopped and rubbed his hands. "Of course not." This was hard. "There are reasons to take prisoners places. Court appearances. Depositions."

"And saving ten thousand lives."

"There will be a reason, I won't break the law. I'll think of something, I'll get you out." He led the way to the door. "Don't screw this up."

I saw myself in the glass of the door. I hated my image. "Do I have to wear these clothes? I'm tired of prison orange."

He veered past a shelf and grabbed a small package that contained the clothes I'd worn when I was arrested. They were clean and neat. In minutes, I was changed and ready for freedom.

Instead I got a patch slapped onto the back of my neck. It was similar to the comunit but instead of a cute, multi-colored Destiny tattoo this one was an ugly black bar code. "Don't force me to use this." He loomed over me as he strapped a small device around his wrist. "I can now find you anywhere and you won't like it if I push this button."

"I'm only interested in saving lives."

He gave the deputy orders regarding the remaining prisoners and said he didn't know how long we'd be gone so not to worry about us. Then he shoved me ahead of him and we left the jailhouse, retracing our original path through a tunnel to the government building rotunda and then outside into the central part of Center City, the heart of the Destiny.

Only after so long in jail, I didn't see a ship. I

needed and wanted and saw and felt sunshine. I turned my face upwards and didn't care that it was from a fake sun. I looked around and felt the joy of people moving freely among buildings that rose tall and straight into the sky. The Destiny was no longer a ship. It was a country and Center City was the capital, complete with streets and parks and it was beautiful.

Okay, maybe the parks weren't beautiful. When I'd had enough sunshine and looked around, I realized that they weren't so lovely. Leaves hung listless and the grass had the look of late summer when it's going dormant. But nothing should go dormant on the Destiny because every living plant had been programmed to be continuously verdant. There was work for me in those parks, a lot of work and I'd best get started. I strode towards the trees.

And was stopped by a hand on my shoulder. "Food is the first concern." He pointed me towards the greenhouses.

"You remember what happened last time we went there."

"Things are different now."

"The botanists are bureaucrats. Bureaucrats don't change."

He knew I was right. "Where then?"

"The orchard where I used to live. My orchard."

"Why that particular one? There are dozens of orchards on the Destiny. Hundreds maybe." Suspicion flared, one hand moved towards the button that could do unspeakable horrors.

"Because I know that orchard. Because it's

probably the healthiest one on the Destiny. Because it'll respond fastest."

His hand dropped, and he led the way to the electric Harley with the Security insignia on the side. It was parked beneath an oak tree with leaves already turning brown. As we passed beneath, I reached up to touch a branch and closed my eyes, hoping Cullen would let me do my thing without pressing that button but knowing that I needed to do this, to help this one tree no matter the consequence. Because it was there, and it was hurting.

When I opened my eyes, his hands were free and, though his whole body was tense, he knew what I was doing. We waited to see how bad the damage was. How hard it would be to bring the Destiny back to life.

In what I felt as a huge sigh, but Cullen probably heard as a breeze, the tree came back. The leaves turned a healthy green and the trunk stood tall once more with branches lifting towards the sky. Cullen watched with no expression. But he waited patiently with me until the tree was as green as Ireland in the spring and as tall as a dwarf oak can be.

Then he waved for me to climb onto the Harley behind him. From that position I could easily conk him on the head and escape and he knew that but still he let me sit there.

I reached out to several fields as we passed to let them know that help was on the way but our passage was too swift to see if my message was received. Then we reached the orchard. My orchard. We stepped off of the Harley and the orchard woke up almost instantly.

"The cherry tree and the tomato plant weren't flukes." Cullen stared at me as if seeing me for the first time. Or as if I had two heads. "You really can do something."

"It's a family thing. Goes way back."

"If you can do this to all the crops the Captain might commute your sentence."

"He might? *Might?* Is that all? I save ten thousand lives and he *might* consider not sending me out the airlock?"

"It's his call, not mine."

I refused to look at Cullen for the rest of that afternoon as we left the now-thriving orchard and headed back to check out the fields we'd passed earlier. As I'd hoped, they were slowly coming back to life. Cullen wagged his head from side to side though, again, he said nothing, just gave me a strange stare. I guess I'm hard to get used to. Then, glancing skyward, he checked the time because what passed for sunshine on the Destiny was dimming. Night was coming fast. "Can you work in the dark?"

"Of course, I can, but I'm tired. This is hard. "

"If you're alive and able to function, we keep going. You can sleep later."

"Is it that bad? The rest of the Destiny?" His lips pressed tightly together said all I needed to know, but I knew what he didn't. "The Destiny is huge. What I can do in one night will hardly make a dent."

He didn't like that. He looked around. Here and there small pockets of healthy plants stood out against the drab, gray-green of the remaining cropland. Seeing them, he brightened. "We can't fix everything immediately but we can go for a psychological lift. People are beginning to panic so even small areas coming back to life might do wonders for morale."

We spent most of that night going from one place to another, each chosen by Cullen for maximum visual impact. By the time I was too tired to help even one more plant, numerous areas of healthy cropland dotted the landscape.

"Do I have to sleep in jail?" Not that it would matter. I was so tired I could easily have slept on the super hard faux dirt. But I'd been in jail for a long time. Too long.

"We're not far from your apartment."

"I promise not to escape."

"I'll make sure you don't. I'll be there too."

I moved slowly, wearily to his bike and climbed on the back. Crawled was more like it because turning an entire ecosystem away from death and towards life had done me in. I wondered if anyone in my family had ever faced a task so daunting. I doubted it because there had always been many family members available for any job. Now there was just me. And the bulk of the work lay ahead.

Cullen tipped my face up, his touch surprisingly gentle. If there'd been a moon, he'd have been silhouetted against it. I thought about that and wondered what he'd look like with the moon as backlighting. Then he spoke in a slightly guilty voice. "You look awful. Why didn't you say something?"

"You were right when you said people need hope. I wanted to get as much done as possible." He climbed in front of me and I practically fell against his back as I waited for him to start. Instead, he got off and moved me in front, cradling me with his arms. I heard his low mutter before I fell asleep. "Can't have you falling off. We need you."

We traveled through the deepening dark until we reached New Rochelle. I think we did, I might have been asleep except I kind of remember the feel of his arms and his solid body and the fresh night air curling around us both.

He parked his bike and half dragged me to my apartment. When we stepped through the door, it was like coming home and the familiarity of the place revived me momentarily. It was a homecoming. My plants were all there, healthy and glowing and glad I was back. "Alicia must have watered them." I yawned.

"Unlike every other plant on the Destiny, these are healthy."

"I'm working on strains that will thrive in this environment." I touched a floribunda rose bush. "You can eat rose petals."

"But that's not why you like it."

I flushed. He was right. It was gorgeous, and I'd made a special project of the bush. I'd not seen many flowers on the Destiny. Practicality was rampant but flowers are nice. I decided I'd check it closer in the morning. At the moment, I was exhausted and only wanted to sleep. The plants understood, they quieted down.

Cullen took the miniature roses from my hand and smelled them. "Nice." Then he put it down and turned all stern and businesslike. "Morning comes early. Get some sleep."

Somehow, I found my bedroom and then my bed. I fell across it, uncaring that I was fully dressed. I thought Cullen pulled a blanket over me but I was too tired to know for sure.

In the morning, as soon as I awoke I visited all of my plants, not just the rose bush. They were doing well and Cullen was gone, my extra bedding folded neatly on one end of the couch. As I stood, uncertain what to do next, a booted foot kicked the door open and Cullen entered, uniform fresh though I couldn't imagine how that could be and arms laden with breakfast. "I fixed your coffee the way you like it. Two sugars and one cream."

"You noticed how I like coffee?"

"It's my job to notice details." He turned away to put breakfast on the table. I couldn't tell if his face really turned red or if it was the morning light that made it seem so. He'd brought croissants. My favorite. And cold cuts, lots of them. "For energy. Busy day ahead."

He was right about that. Having dotted the Destiny with patches of thriving, growing, living crops the previous day to give people hope, that morning we started the grueling work of bringing the entire huge farm that was the Destiny up to snuff. Our plan was to head for the back end and work our way towards the front. We did just that though it took almost eight weeks to get everything back to normal. But, by the end of the last week, the Destiny was once again the thriving, happy world it had been when it pulled away from Earth and headed into the unknown.

All that time Cullen slept on my couch and it must have been uncomfortable because he was about a foot taller than it was long. He watched my plants with what I finally figured out was fear. "You don't like plants?" I tried to be tactful.

He hunched forward to avoid touching a lovely carrot growing in a small glass of water. "I grew up mostly on space shuttles. Not many plants around." And a very small space most likely. Which was why he didn't like cramped places. In the following days I noticed that he came to a wary agreement with my plants. He didn't stomp on them and they ignored him. It worked to a degree. Eventually, about the time I felt comfortable and rested, we stared at one another across the breakfast table with nothing more that needed doing. It was time to face the future.

I started the conversation. "I'm still a stowaway."

"Yes." He coughed and looked away. Found himself staring at the floribunda rose bush and back quickly because he hadn't yet come to terms with something that existed mostly to be beautiful. Space shuttles are utilitarian vehicles. "You are a stowaway and that must be dealt with."

"So what happens now?"

He looked me straight in the eyes though I suspected it was one of the hardest things he'd ever done. The tiny lines at the corners of his eyes were deeper, more noticeable and there were lines on either side of his mouth that I'd not seen before. "I wish I could say that everything will be all right but I won't lie. It's the Captain's call and no matter how severe your punishment is I won't be able to alter it. Furthermore, it'll be my job to carry out your sentence." As he said those last words, he finally looked away. My future could be worse than even Cullen Vail was willing to admit. "But I don't have to bring your case to the Captain right away. I can put it off a while."

Which made me feel worse than ever. What kind of person was the Captain? What would my punishment be?

Chapter Nine

I didn't sleep that night. I thought about escaping. I suspected that Cullen would pretend to be asleep if I slipped past his bulk on the couch, but I didn't even try. At first I didn't know why I stayed where I was, but as I thought about it, I knew.

I was done hiding. Done running. Done being a felon. In some distant recess of my mind, I figured I'd done my best, I'd saved the Destiny, and if that wasn't good enough to warrant a light sentence, then neither the Captain nor the people on the Destiny deserved my continued work on their behalf.

And they would need me again. Crops would fail again because they always do now and then and eventually the problem would once again be so severe that nothing would keep them alive if I wasn't around. If I escaped and hid, then I'd be there when that time came, and I could save them. It's what my family has done for thousands of years. Hide and help.

But I was alone. More to the point, I was tired and beyond caring. I stayed where I was and we had croissants and coffee and sausage for breakfast as we'd done every morning since I left jail and Cullen kept his word and didn't immediately mention me to the Captain.

So it was another week before word got to the Captain in a roundabout way that there was a stowaway on board who needed to be dealt with. With the plants healthy, he was no longer unapproachable.

"I told him there was more to the story than just you stowing away. I suggested that you aren't the usual stowaway. I did my best." Cullen raked fingers through his hair. "I don't know if it helped but he does want to meet with you privately instead of on the bridge."

"Thank you." I took a deep breath. "When? Where?"

"Today. Now. In his private quarters."

"That's a good sign, isn't it?"

"I don't know."

I followed Cullen into the Captain's quarters in the largest house in a small community just off the government center. I supposed they were the homes of officials and their families and Cullen said that was right. As we knocked on the door, I wasn't afraid. I couldn't figure out why not until I realized that I was resigned and past the point of caring.

The Captain was in his living room in a huge easy chair that rather resembled a throne. He wasn't the grizzled old man I thought all captains must be. Instead, he was middle-aged though I suspected that his wife, who was hanging around pretending not to watch while she took everything in, was quite a bit younger.

She was pretty, all brown hair and eyes and soft

skin and lots of rings on her fingers and toes that showed through the skimpy sandals she wore. She looked like an artist and seemed like a nice person, not at all the kind who'd marry a grumpy old man. But I thought she might be the kind who'd fall in love with a dashing Captain and stand by his side as he guided a ship on a one-way journey through space. She smiled at me as we entered. The Captain didn't.

Neither did he ignore us. In a bored way, he indicated that we sit so we did, on a couch, Cullen by my side, stiff and official and not touching me while the Captain leaned back in his chair and steepled his fingers.

"So you're the stowaway." I nodded. "But Cullen here seems to think I should be lenient." He moved then and leaned towards me, bushy brows hiding sharp, intelligent eyes above a hawk-like nose and a sharp chin. "Can't figure out why, which is why I asked to see you here. Cullen is the epitome of law-abiding citizenry, the upholder of the law, the keeper of the peace." The Captain watched for my reaction but I was careful to give nothing away. "So, when this paragon of legal virtue pleads for leniency on behalf of a felon of no particular value, I'm curious. Why does he speak up for you?

"I know it's not love or even lust because our Cullen here would never let either get in the way of duty. He lives and breathes duty. So I want you to tell me what's going on. Why he thinks you are special." Still leaning forward, he put his hands on his knees while his wife, in the background, moved closer in order to hear better. "So start talking."

I told him about my family. "We go back a long way. Thousands of years."

"So does everyone."

"We trace our ancestors to ancient Greece and Rome."

"Do tell." He was losing interest. I saw myself being sent out the airlock.

"One of those ancestors was Ceres. Another was Demeter."

Those bushy brows knitted until they touched over the bridge of his nose. "If I remember my mythology correctly, you are talking about the goddesses of the harvest."

"You know your history."

"Not history. Mythology because that's what Ceres and Demeter are. Myths. Legends."

"They were real people." He snorted in disbelief but he didn't stop listening. He'd promised to hear me out and he would do so. "And what they did was real. When crops were failing, they stepped in and saved them. In the process, they saved the lives of everyone who depended on those crops."

He sliced a hand through the air to shut me up. He knew where this was going and didn't like having been conned into listening to garbage. "Myths don't save lives. Legends don't save people."

"Ceres and Demeter weren't legends and neither am I. They saved lives by protecting the crops all those years ago and I saved the people of the Destiny in the last several weeks by saving the crops that were dying."

"Preposterous." From the corner of my eye I noticed the Captain's wife creep closer and at mention of Demeter and Ceres, those brown eyes opened wide. This was a juicy story and she would hear and remember every word. Did she and the wives of the other officers have tea in the houses we'd passed? Did they gossip as they sipped Chamomile with lemon and sugar?

The Captain was the only person whose opinion was important, though, and he didn't believe me. No one ever did and just like everyone who'd heard our story he dismissed it out of hand as if I'd not said a word. "The botanists saved the crops. Our wonderfully talented and very pampered scientists figured out what was wrong and fixed it."

Cullen coughed to get the Captain's attention. "The greenhouses are full of dead and dying plants."

"Really?" The Captain's attention was diverted to Cullen for a moment, but only a moment. "Even if that's true it doesn't prove a thing. Of course they would concern themselves with the harvest first. If that meant ignoring their experiments for a while, then that's what they'd do."

His attention was fast fading and he was growing restless. Not so his wife but she knew better than to interrupt her husband. In one last desperate move, Cullen blurted out, "She can prove that what she says is true."

The Captain turned back to me, still bored, still unbelieving. "Can you?" I nodded. "How?"

Cullen put his hand on mine to quiet me so he could talk. He knew the Captain, he knew what would convince him. "She brought a sick tomato plant back to health in front of my eyes. It took less than a minute and I saw her do the same for every single crop on the Destiny."

"I can't believe you expected me to listen to such a ridiculous story."

Cullen looked around. "Do you have any sick plants?"

"I do." The Captain's wife disappeared in another room and then reappeared soon after with an African violet. I knew by the way she held it that she liked growing things. That was good to know.

But it was almost dead. There was no sign of a blossom and I knew that there hadn't been for a long time. What should have been lovely, soft greenery hung limply. It was well cared for and normally that would have been enough but now, on the Destiny, in the middle of deep space and in the strangeness of a space ship, it needed something more. It needed me and the special bond that my family has with green and growing things. To tell it that things were all right. To get it past the fear of the unknown. It had food and water but that hadn't been enough.

I took the violet and closed my eyes. Then I did what I'd been trained to do, what I'd felt in me while a child and that had been honed by both my family and my education. But I did more. I did the exact opposite of what my family had taught me to do. I brought that African violet back to life and health in record time and

I did it in front of an audience of non-believers. I did it because my freedom... possibly my very life... and the lives of the entire Destiny complement of people... depended on my doing so.

When I opened my eyes, the violet was once more a beautiful accessory with several colorful blossoms that the Captain's wife put on a small table in a corner where it set off the whole room in the lovely way. Her private smile said she liked pretty things and enjoyed decorating her home. She was an artist.

As her hands, with all those rings, left the violet she turned to her husband. "She did what she said she'd do." It was the first words she'd said. Her voice was low and husky and somehow lovely. And lonely though I couldn't know what she was lonely for.

"That's one plant. Not much of a demonstration."

Cullen rose and pulled me up too. "Come to the greenhouse. It's full of sick plants."

It wasn't far, and the botanists didn't appreciate an unannounced visit. But, as the head grower pointed out, though the plants in the greenhouse were still sickly, the rest of the crops on the Destiny were vibrant and so heavy with abundance that the workers were having a hard time keeping up.

The Captain glanced at me. "How'd you guys do it? How'd you cure whatever was wrong?"

The moment the head grower licked his lips and wrung his hands to give himself time to come up with a believable answer, the Captain knew they'd not saved the crops. I had. But one African violet wasn't enough, he needed more proof. "We're going to take a look around. None of you should come with us. I'm sure you have things to do. Plants to grow. Experiments to continue."

The scientists weren't happy. They suggested we wait until they had the greenhouse back to normal before taking our tour. They told us we'd be disappointed because they'd been too busy outside the greenhouses to attend to the plants inside. They said all kinds of things and the more they said the less the Captain believed them.

"I feel like taking a couple of my friends through the greenhouses and we're going now." The scientists melted away as he walked through them, pulling Cullen and me along. Soon we were back in the tomato house where Cullen once got his uniform wet and where he'd found a sickly plant for me to revive. The whole place looked awful. My heart sank as I surveyed the dead and dying plants. I could help some of them, but there was no help for most of them.

The Captain stopped as he took in the state of the plants and sort of caught his breath. "Think you can do something?"

At least he asked. He knew most were beyond help. "Some of them can be saved."

He picked up a small plant that wasn't as bad as most. "This one?"

"I think so."

He handed it to me and folded his arms. "Okay. I'm waiting."

It was a nice plant, one of several hybrids the scientists had been working on. As I closed my eyes and let my mind drift to that place I access when near green things I realized that they'd been on the right track. Given enough time they might have developed strains that would grow in deep space. But there hadn't been enough time.

When I opened my eyes, the plant was healthy again and there were several tiny, green tomatoes along the branches. The Captain took it back and turned it over and over, examining it closely. "If I hadn't seen it with my own eyes, I'd never have believed it."

"This plant is a new kind. The scientists were doing their best and they were close. They would have figured it out eventually."

"In time to save our lives?"

"No."

He put the tomato plant back and led the way to the other greenhouses. In each place, I brought one or more plants back to health. By the time we'd gone through every greenhouse and were finishing the circle that brought us back to the offices, the Captain was a believer. "Cullen was right. We need you."

"I promise to do my best."

Those grizzled eyebrows rose. "If?"

"You let me go free." My lips were stiff, it was hard to speak but this was important.

"Then you're free."

For a long time I couldn't say a single word. Then I said simply, "Thank you."

If we continued, we'd be back with the scientists in moments but the Captain held out an arm to stop us.

"Free, but with conditions."

"Such as?" Any conditions at all, I almost said, as long as they don't involve an airlock with me in it. But I kept my head about me and asked what the conditions were and tried to sound like I was negotiating terms when actually I was giving thanks.

"You did stow away and that's a felony. There were mitigating circumstances, I admit, you do happen to have an essential ability... a trick... that we didn't know we needed. But we do. So I'm glad you're aboard and I acknowledge your importance to the continued health of the people under my charge.

"But you missed out on the usual background searches and psychological testing applicants were put through. You're an unknown quantity and that could be a problem, not to mention that all the colonists who did go through that rigorous screening might resent you just waltzing on board and they might not be as nice as I'm being right now. In fact, they might not be nice at all.

"I've heard the gossip. There are people on board who think those chosen as colonists are the best of the best and they aren't shy about saying so and I've seen fights break out over whose genes are the most superior.

"So. I want to know where you are and what you're doing at all times and I'm charging Cullen with the task of keeping track of you and keeping you safe."

Cullen nodded. "I'll get my best men on it. She'll have someone with her twenty-four seven."

The Captain shook his head. "Not your best men.

You. I want you to keep her safe."

Cullen's mouth dropped open. "Me? Just me? Twenty-four seven? How can I manage that?"

"That's your problem. Move her in with you. Move in with her. Do what you have to do. Drag her along whenever you go. Follow her everywhere. I don't care how you keep tabs on her, just so long as you do, and you do it yourself. No one else will believe what we just saw so you're elected."

"I have a job."

"You're the most compulsively organized person I know. Security runs like clockwork, thanks to you. Which means that your presence isn't necessary."

Cullen had nothing to say except, "Yes sir."

We were at the door to the main room. The scientists were beyond, awaiting our return. Their faces were anxious. I tugged at the Captain's sleeve. "If it's all right with you, Sir, I'd rather as few people as possible know about my … er … gift."

"Why?" His huge head hung over mine and his eyes held the fierce gaze of an eagle.

"Because whenever people find out about us, bad things happen."

"Like witches being burned?"

"And other things."

He nodded. "I understand. It'll be our little secret." He thumped Cullen on the back. "You'll come up with some story as to why you're stuck to her like glue."

Cullen wilted. "People will think we're having an affair."

"Good idea. Simple and believable. In fact it's

perfect. Everyone has been wondering about you. No social life, no girlfriend. There have been questions, believe me. Now those questions will be answered." He thumped him again. "Even if the answer is a lie."

He examined me again. "You're not a bad-looking woman and you seem intelligent and I know you are educated." Up and down, head to toe, with that eagle eye. "So, now that I know your story, I'm wondering. Why go to all the trouble of stowing away? Why didn't you just apply to be a colonist?"

I licked my lips and hoped my answer didn't send me out that airlock after all. "We tired. Lots of us applied but we were all turned down."

"You look healthy to me."

"Applicants were screened for genetic diseases and abnormalities. Our genes are unusual. Different. Abnormal. So our applications were refused."

"And it's that abnormality that gives you your gift?"

"Yes."

He nodded that he understood and dropped his hand from the door that separated us from the scientists who were ready to pounce the instant they got me alone. He glared at Cullen. "I don't want anything to happen to this young lady. She's unique, one of a kind, and evidently, we need her. Make sure everyone thinks you two are having an affair or whatever you decide will do the trick."

Cullen's hand was on my arm, ready to propel me through the door the instant it opened. The Captain took a step back, examined the two of us and grimaced. "If an affair is to be your cover, Cullen, you'd best do more than touch this young lady as if she were an insect. You'd best work hard to convince everyone that the two of you are lovers. Give them a reason to accept her and make it good. If that's going to be your cover."

He pushed open the door to the scientists, who were anxiously awaiting his comments on their greenhouses. He didn't disappoint them, towering over them though physically he wasn't taller as he said, "Pretty sad what I saw back there."

To a man, they cringed. "We were busy with the crops in the fields. We planned to get around to the greenhouses when we could."

The Captain pointed to me. "This lady has a degree in botany. She isn't busy, and you are. I'm assigning her to the greenhouses as soon as she can get out of her current job."

"When will she be available?" The head grower tried to look happy while sending daggers in my direction.

The Captain smiled so broadly that everyone knew he'd caught that nasty look and was ignoring it because he knew no one would dare flaunt his wishes. "How soon do you think, Elle?" I was under his protection and they'd better not touch a hair on my head.

"I have to give notice and train a replacement." As if harvesting apples required lessons. But I was determined to put off my employment in the greenhouses as long as possible.

Once outside, we found the Captain's wife on the sidewalk, all dressed up, young and lovely and in love with her important husband. He groaned under his breath and said, "I forgot. I promised to meet Darlene for lunch. Guess your little demonstration sent everything else out of my mind." He waved to her and she came close and tipped her head in question. "Yes, Darlene, she's the real deal."

Darlene stared at me in awe and, propelled by her husband who wanted to get her away from me and my abnormal genes as soon as possible, they disappeared in the direction of one of the more elegant restaurants in the government center, leaving Cullen and me staring at each other.

He didn't know what to do. He gazed longingly after the premier couple on the Destiny as he backed away a couple of feet. Then he remembered that we were supposed to be lovers and drew close again, tentatively putting an arm across my shoulders. His fingers barely touched my shirt.

"If that's the best you can do no one will believe we're lovers." The arm came around me more closely. "You call that progress? I look like a prisoner." I shrugged until his arm slid across my shoulder and his fingers touched my neck.

"I wish you were a prisoner. I know how to deal with prisoners."

"Well I'm free. Captain's orders."

"I know." He sighed, a sound pulled from his toes. He looked so woeful that I had the insane urge to soothe his brow but I didn't. Instead, I remembered that we were supposed to be lovers, so I reached up and stroked his forehead with a touch as light as a feather. Then I planted a kiss on his cheek.

My gesture was clearly not sexual. But as my fingers left his forehead and my lips left his cheek, I pulled back, stunned by my body's reaction to that feather touch. I felt splintered into a thousand pieces. I actually looked down to be sure I was still there.

As for Cullen, he kind of cocked his head and tried to pretend the kiss was okay. To smile, even, but I saw in his face that it was hard for him not to brush me away like a pesky fly.

Chapter Ten

That got me angry. How dare he think of me as an insect! My muscles tensed in preparation for slugging him as hard as I knew how. Then I stopped. We were supposed to be lovers so instead of slapping him across his face, I stood on my tiptoes and kissed him again. And again, all the time knowing that no matter how he hated what was happening, he'd not dare do anything about it.

There were several people nearby, going about their business. They paused to watch so, as Cullen loomed over me and I made sure that our kiss lasted as long as possible I could almost feel the rumors spread out from that sidewalk to the farthest reaches of the Destiny, through every field and orchard and nook and cranny and maybe beyond, into outer space. Cullen Vail and Elle Olmstead were an item.

And as the kiss went on an on, I was blown to smithereens again but this time I didn't check myself to make sure I was still intact because I knew the disintegration wasn't physical. But as I finally pulled away, I was disgusted that a simple kiss could affect me so profoundly. Me, Elle Olmstead, woman of intelligence and many degrees who knew ease and comfort and exactly what the world was like and where in it I belonged.

Problem was, I wasn't on that world any longer.

I leaned back and looked up into those night eyes. I pecked him again on the cheek just to show that I was the one in control. "We put on a good show, didn't we?"

His arms were steel and held me tight as one dark eyebrow rose at my words and he fought to get his breathing back under control. Good! At least he wasn't totally immune to me.

But he hadn't splintered like I had. His lips twitched complacently leaving me to hope I matched his self-control. "Guess we should go now." He dumped me and started away, long legs striding in double-time, leaving me to find my balance as best I could. "Got to figure how to fit your things in my house."

He wasn't heading for either the elevators or his bike. He was heading for the houses where the important people on the Destiny lived. Of course, it would be where the head of Security was housed. I yelled after him, uncaring who heard. "I will not live in Center City."

"Yes you will." The nearby watchers turned towards us in order to hear better. Yep, the gossip mill was in high gear. "My job is in Center City so we live in my house."

"I hate cities." He snorted and kept walking. The watchers held their breath over this fascinating lovers' quarrel. I cringed thinking of the story about to make the rounds. Then I ran after Cullen and whispered so none of them could hear. "I'll lose my powers if I stay here." I do work best in the country, that was true even if the rest was a bit of an exaggeration.

"You're lying. You won't lose them." His own voice was low enough to keep the conversation between the two of us though a woman nearby held her breath in an attempt to hear better.

"I will." I put my lips to his ear. Nuzzled him, let my lips drift over the skin behind his ear, knowing what any onlookers would make of my gesture, fighting my body's reaction because I didn't want to come apart a third time in one day. "My gift doesn't come easy. I can't just wave my arms and make everything right. I have to concentrate, and I can't do that when I'm tired or tense and I'm both in a city. The noise drives me crazy not to mention that there's a dearth of plants here."

"There's green, living stuff all over the Destiny. Almost every square inch." He didn't move, didn't turn to me, did nothing to stop my lips from grazing his neck. I breathed deeply and licked his skin, gratified by his sudden intake of breath. "There are plants in Center City." He inclined his head enough to indicate a nearby park. "Look around."

"No matter how lovely, it's still a city. I'm a country girl."

He turned and as simply as that our lips were almost touching. "What do you consider country on the Destiny?" He saw the Destiny as a ship, I saw it as a self-contained world, complete with meadows, forests and towns. "Where, exactly, do you need to be in order to do what you do?"

I brightened. I was about to get what I needed. Wanted. "Home. The orchard. Or my apartment in New Rochelle."

He rolled his eyes and shuddered. "A small town. A tiny apartment."

"Surrounded by farms and orchards."

His wiggled his shoulders. Stared at me. Scowled. Gave up because he couldn't prove I wasn't truthful. "Okay." He pulled back a few inches. Our lovers' quarrel evidently settled, people around us moved on about their business but I knew their comunits were working overtime spreading the word that Cullen Vail had a girlfriend. "I need some things, clothes, stuff like that. It won't take long." He started off but turned when I didn't follow. "Come on"

"I'll wait here."

"You can't do that. We're joined at the hip, remember?" Then he did something unexpected. He smiled, a slight flexing of facial muscles that looked to onlookers like a real smile but that told me he was about to get back at me for our very public kiss. "We're supposed to be lovers. What's more natural than for the two of us to disappear into my place for a while?"

My face flamed but I trudged beside him to a building that was smaller than the ones around it but still imposing and then he led the way on up the porch steps.

His house was spare, with little furniture and no pictures of family or friends so there were few things for him to stuff into the backpacks he pulled from under his bed. He filled one with clothes and tossed it aside, then filled the second with still more clothes and a few personal care items. He started to close it. Then he stopped.

I pretended to look out the window while surreptitiously watching to see what he'd almost forgotten. Cullen Vail never forgot anything. I almost lost my breath when he pulled a set of lovely, handmade pan pipes from a drawer and placed them quickly into the bag, wrapping them in several layers of clothes to keep them safe, all the while looking my way to see if I'd noticed. I stared hard out the window so he'd not know I was watching.

He was the musician in the orchard. Seeing the pipes, I had no doubt and the knowledge knocked me speechless. He was the man whose music had moved me. The magical shadow who took me back to Earth and all I held dear. Cullen Vail, man of no emotion, had made the music that had brought me to tears and laughter.

But he didn't want anyone to know. He'd slipped into an orchard he'd thought deserted and only played his pipes in the middle of the night. Because he was the head of Security, a man of no emotion, an armed policeman capable of doing whatever it took to keep order.

I continued to pretend to look out the window at the city beyond as inside of me everything I'd known about Cullen Vail changed. Morphed. I stared at buildings and people but I was seeing the orchard at night and the outline of a mysterious man playing love songs.

He, of course, thought I was watching a slice of city life through his window. He closed his backpacks and joined me warily, afraid for a moment that I'd jump on him, but I didn't so together we looked at the scene beyond the window while I managed to avoid staring at the backpack with great effort. And I tried to think of something to say. Anything. "I hope you don't mess up your job because of moving to New Rochelle."

He shrugged. "No problem. I can live anywhere. I can keep in touch from every corner of the Destiny."

"Unlike what you told the captain."

"I told the captain the truth. My job is here, things would go better if I stayed in my own house."

"I hope you can manage."

"I can." His voice wasn't strident any longer. It was quiet, soft almost. Human.

I was close enough to see the dark hairs on the backs of his hands. I turned slightly to see the rest of him, this man who was suddenly an unknown quantity. It was an odd feeling. He was the same man as five minutes earlier and yet he was entirely different and all because of the pan pipes. He stood stiff as I made myself continue with more small talk, blurting out the only thing I could think of. "I'm sorry you have to watch me yourself. I'm sorry I'm such a bother."

His answering look sent a bolt of electricity through me head to toe and back again. "I'm just doing my job." He stared at me and licked his lips. Then, as if he couldn't stop himself, he took a step until we were almost touching, and I could see that his eyes now, unlike other times, were all the colors of a living, breathing night. "And right now you are my job, Elle Olmstead. You. Just you."

If I touched him ... just touched him ... my insides would skitter in every direction and I'd come totally apart from the strain of trying to fit the two completely different people he'd become into one body. I stayed still and stared at him from a distance of a few inches.

He cleared his throat again but his voice was still scratchy as if he was catching a cold. "We should get going."

We left his house and climbed onto his bike and set off with me behind him and my arms around his waist. I was glad for the layers of clothing separating our bodies.

It was soon apparent that he didn't like my apartment. "It's not like when you were doing whatever it was that you did to bring the crops back to health. Then I knew I wouldn't be here long." He sighed, ran his fingers through that black hair until it was actually tousled. Then he pointed at my couch with a look of pure hate. "But I refuse to sleep on that thing any longer than necessary."

I offered him my bed but he refused. Of course. So, when I crawled into my comfortable bed several hours later, I pictured him scrunched on my couch and I felt so guilty that I couldn't sleep because he was forced to watch out for me and that meant that he was sleeping on a couch a foot shorter than he was.

I wiggled a few times and deliberately thought

about kittens and pink clouds, but I still couldn't sleep. I tried one side and then the other but that didn't help either. I checked the time on my comunit and groaned. The night was passing. In the morning Cullen would take one look at me and think that being in my own apartment wasn't helping and he'd insist we live in Center City. I didn't want that.

So I picked up a pillow and threw it across the room to vent a little frustration. It hit the wall with a thud as Braveheart scrambled as far from me as possible and mewed loudly. I silently apologized to Braveheart for scaring him but throwing the pillow had felt good.

"You okay in there?"

"I'm fine."

"I heard something."

"My pillow fell on the floor."

"Pillows don't make that kind of noise unless they are thrown."

I blew hair from my eyes. It was growing out, had grown a lot since I'd cut it and the brown dye had faded during my incarceration until I was now almost back to my original bright orange, insanely curly, long hair. I'd felt Cullen's gaze on it several times and once he'd said something about not needing a light at night. It was hard to pull fingers through those curls but I was so frustrated that I managed, yanking out a few hairs in the process. "Okay, it didn't fall. I threw it."

Silence, then, "I'm sorry that you wish I was elsewhere. But I'm staying."

Time for truth. Sort of. Not the whole truth but I

did appreciate the fact that he was nearby. "I'm not angry with you."

He sighed so loudly that I heard it through the wall. "Liar." His baritone penetrated the walls easily. "As far as you are concerned, I'm the devil incarnate."

I padded across the bedroom and reassured Bravehart that I didn't hate him, then I retrieved my pillow and brought it back to my bed where I curled around it, telling myself I shouldn't feel the need to apologize to someone who'd throw me out of the airlock if the Captain so ordered. "You're not the devil." It was easy to hate Cullen Vail, head of Security. It was harder to hate someone who played pipes in the middle of the night and made music that filled my heart to bursting.

Not just harder, it was impossible.

The first thought I had the next morning as I uncoupled myself from that pillow and cuddled Braveheart until he butted me with his head and left my bedroom was that Cullen would make some lucky woman a wonderful housewife, a thought I'd had every morning during the time when I'd done my thing with the plants on the Destiny and come home exhausted each night. As on those mornings, today the table was set for two and I saw muffins and fruit on it. Breakfast smells wafted from the stove where sausage and eggs were being kept warm. I could use someone like Cullen around the house.

Cullen was eating his food with gusto, wide awake. He was a morning person. "I went for a walk already." He shoved a plate at me. "I ran into Wilkes Zander. We talked."

"About what?" I ignored the table, found a muffin and slathered it with jam, wandering the room as I ate while Cullen remained at the table with a full plate.

"He's getting us a different apartment. One with two bedrooms."

I couldn't argue with that even though I'd turned my apartment into a comfortable home. "Where is the new place?"

"Close. An apartment down the hall happens to be vacant."

I licked jam from my fingers. "When?"

"Today. The movers will do everything, we just have to get out of their way."

We looked at his backpacks in a corner. One was closed, the other open where he'd dug in it for clothes. Braveheart was checking them out, weaving around them. "We can go to the orchard while we wait. It's time to harvest apples." Kittens like to crawl inside things. I started after Braveheart before he slipped into Cullen's backpack.

Too late. He was in it and mewing happily. Cullen panicked. "Get out of there!" He moved to drag Braveheart out but the kitten was slippery. Instead of removing Braveheart, Cullen knocked the backpack over and the contents spilled onto the floor, including the pan pipes.

They skittered across the rug with Braveheart in pursuit and Cullen not far behind. "Hey, cat! Leave them alone!" He grabbed them and held them high while he stared suspiciously at Braveheart. "Leave my pipes alone."

"They are beautiful." He froze as I said the words because they meant that I saw the pipes, possibly the first person ever. He was white with some emotion I couldn't understand but I knew that I had to say something, had to get him moving again, had to get him past whatever fear he had of people knowing he was a talented musician. I blurted out the story of my aunt. "She made her own pipes. Did you make yours?"

"I won them in a poker game."

"I bet you play beautifully."

"I don't play. I liked the look of them, that's all, so I kept them."

We stared at one another. He dared me to argue farther and I knew he'd never acknowledge his ability. I changed the topic. "It's going to be a busy day. There are apples in the orchard ready to be harvested and since we're joined at the hip, you're about to be educated on the finer points of picking fruit." I pointedly ignored the expression on his face. "Got a pair of heavy, cotton work gloves?"

He didn't need them, of course, but I made him get some from the store in town so people would think we harvested crops the same way everyone else did. By hand instead of by conversing with the trees and bushes and convincing them to gently lay their fruit in my cart. When I suggested he rub the gloves on a few trunks to get them dirty, he did so with a dazed expression. I tried to make him feel better. "You're not the only one who feels odd about this situation."

"Odd?" He stared at his gloved hands. "Is that

what you call talking to trees? Odd? Even odder is that they listen and do what you want."

"I told you it's a gift."

He leaned one hip against the cart and took an apple and turned it every which way as if doing so would help him figure me out. "I wish I knew how it works."

I sank to the ground, crossing my legs as I went downward until I sat easily between a lovely apple tree and the cart it had proudly deposited apples in. And I tried to explain something no one in my family had ever explained before. "Think of the orchard as an orchestra. The trees want to make the best music possible and they are wonderful individually but they need someone to coordinate their efforts. To show them how to produce the best music ... the best apples ... possible. I know a lot about growing things so I have a lot of ideas and they listen to me."

"You're a botanist."

"I have a degree in botany and that helps, but mostly it's intuition."

"Like any good music depends on the ability of the musician as much as on their training."

"Exactly. So now you understand."

"Except for the fact that most people can't talk to trees. Or understand their language."

"There is that."

"You were born with that ability."

"It's the gene thing. My abnormal genetic makeup."

"The reason none of you were accepted as

colonists."

Instead of answering, I leaned back and stared at the faux sky that was my new normal. Cullen slid down beside me, and we sat in companionable silence for a while. Companionable? Cullen? I marveled that I was comfortable with him but I enjoyed his silence because I hate people who babble on just for the sake of talking.

I wanted to take his hand but didn't. Saw his hand move towards mine, then move back without touching. And thought about us because suddenly, unexpectedly, it felt like there was an 'us.'

Not Cullen. Not now, not ever. But some part of me kept asking 'if not Cullen, then who?' There was no one besides me on the Destiny with my abilities so marrying within my own kind wasn't an option. And the idea of a popsicle fathering my children made me shudder. So why not Cullen?

I shook my head, shaking the image out of my mind, checked the time, started the engine on the cart and we took our harvest to town where Cullen's presence was followed by stares and whispers much the way the passage of a shark is followed by a wave as it swims through the ocean.

We had lunch at the café with Wilkes Zander and his whole, extended family in what looked like a friendly gathering and was, in reality, a business meeting between the head of Security and the Mayor of New Rochelle, something everyone knew by then and respected. In this new world the colonists were creating, new norms were being created every day.

Meetings were both social and business and it worked.

People gave the two men privacy even as Cullen pulled me close because I was his job and he wasn't about to let me get too far from his protective bulk. That bulk felt pretty good even though I'd just figured out that I should be avoiding him like the plague if I didn't want to find my emotions all tangled up and just being close seemed to do that. As for Cullen, nothing about our relationship was personal. He could do two things at once, hold me in a way that made us look like lovers and discuss business with Wilkes Zander.

I settled down and set about shoving Cullen from my mind as the two men talked. I'd long ago vowed to fall in love carefully because people in my family have power. Lots of power that could do terrible things if used unwisely. I'd never let myself get serious about anyone.

But Cullen Vail was the epitome of responsibility. His children would be intelligent, responsible and stubborn. He was precisely the kind of father my children should have if the colonists were to thrive on whatever planet the Destiny reached. I glanced at him sidewise and pictured him as a patriarch. It was easy.

Then he and Wilkes Zander finished their conversation and the table erupted into conversation because the business part of the meeting was done, and the visiting could commence.

The women asked Cullen what we should wear for the first ever upcoming visit from the Captain. Another meeting that would be both a social visit and an official function. It would be the first ever so no one knew what constituted proper attire. This meeting would set the protocol for all such future meetings so what to wear was important, at least to the women at the table. Cullen said stiffly that he had no idea what women wore.

Alicia's mother finally offered to ask a friend in Center City who knew Darlene Smithers what she planned to wear. We could all take our cues from the captain's wife. Remembering the quiet, artistic woman with an African violet in her hands, I wondered if we'd all end up in long, silky, artist-type dresses and whether the store in town carried such things.

Chapter Eleven

We did indeed wear sheer, long dresses, the kind the nearby store didn't stock because this was a farm town. But Alicia's mom got them for us in a rush trip to Center City. She had our sizes and we trusted her. She returned with a rainbow of colors. Mine was green. "Because you're a redhead and a farmer,"

"I love green," I replied, pretending to like it while thinking back to a childhood of being thrust into green outfits because I'm a redhead. I'd worn enough green to last a lifetime but I sighed and tried it on. Purple would have been lovely, or pink, but green it was.

The official part of the visit went smoothly with the Captain inspecting everything there was to inspect, which wasn't much, and smiling as if he knew what it was used for, which he probably did. Then he and Darleen retired to an empty apartment that had been turned over to them so they could dress for the evening's festivities, a dance in the town square.

Cullen and I changed in my apartment. *Our* apartment because we were joined at the hip. Soon after I was ready Cullen emerged from his bedroom in the stiff, black dress uniform that matched both his demeanor and his dark hair and eyes.

I had something to say, a request to make. I started innocuously. "The plants are healthy, the crisis is past. Everything is normal again."

He flicked an imaginary speck of dust from a sleeve, an unnecessary gesture because no dust would dare sully Cullen Vail's perfect image. "So?"

"So the Destiny is safe and so am I. It's about time you moved back to your house in Center City."

"I'll go when the captain orders me to and not one moment before."

"You could ask him tonight."

He muttered something unintelligible and I swished imperiously around his granite self, trailing green gauze, and headed for the door. He followed and slammed the door hard behind us. But I had made my point and, in the process, came to wonder why I'd ever considered him as father material. The man was impossible.

We reached the town square a little early, my diaphanous dress billowing against his black uniform. "I feel like I'm wearing curtains that should be decorating a window and blowing in the breeze."

"Except on the Destiny there is no wind."

"There should be. A mistake in planning. Plants need wind. It's how they communicate."

"There were no mistakes made when the Destiny was designed." His voice was stiff. "The best minds on earth designed her."

"Huh!"

We couldn't argue further because at that moment the captain and his wife appeared. The pink and white cloud that was Darlene Smithers in an even more diaphanous dress than mine saw me, veered from her husband's arm and made a beeline for us. For me. Her eyes bored into mine, then drifted towards Cullen.

Cullen read Darlene's expression. "She wants to talk to you. Alone." He looked around uncomfortably. "But I stay wherever you are."

I followed his gaze around the town square. "See any thugs who want to snatch me?" I swung my arm wide. "No one is out to get me because I don't need protection." He scowled as I pointed to Captain Smithers watching his wife walk toward us. "The captain isn't busy. You could ask him to rescind his order of protection." I rose to my tiptoes and gave him my most truculent stare. "You can still see us and have your gun drawn in case someone tries to abduct me."

He patted his holster and grunted as Darlene reached us. Stared at him pointedly as she raised one eyebrow and waited for him to leave, knowing that as the captain's wife her slightest wish would be obeyed. Cullen scowled again, gave me a black look that said I'd better not try to ditch him, and then he sauntered a few yards away.

Darlene sniffed. "Your boyfriend is the strong, silent type."

"He's not my boyfriend."

"That's not how it looks to me." She bit her lip to keep from laughing. "Strong and silent isn't a bad kind of man. I'm married to one of the worst, but I suspect Cullen and my husband are identical in that respect." I agreed politely and waited to find out what she wanted. Something was on her mind. Her next words proved me right. "Is there somewhere we can talk? Somewhere private?"

We found a couple of lawn chairs that had been set out for people to watch the dancing. We pulled them a discreet distance from the growing throng. Cullen moved fractionally to keep us in sight and the captain followed. They spoke. I wished I knew what they were saying. Perhaps I would get my wish and Cullen would be reassigned.

Darlene Smithers next words sent all other thoughts from my mind. "I know what you did. I know you saved the Destiny. Not many people know, I'm one of the few who do. You deserve accolades and I thank you for my life and the lives of all of us." I waited. There was more, I knew it and after a long pause, it came. "After that meeting in our house when you brought back my African violet, I looked you up. You and your ancestors. The goddess Ceres. She was your ancestor, goddess of the harvest."

I nodded cautiously as she continued. "There's a lot of information in the Destiny library so I know that wasn't all Ceres could do." My breath slowed as I figured out where this conversation was going. "Ceres did more than make sure the harvest is bountiful." She unconsciously patted her flat stomach and I knew my suspicions were right. "Ceres was also the goddess of fertility."

Darleen looked down at her hands on her stomach. Stared at them. "We are childless." Realizing that I was watching, she withdrew her hands quickly. "We've tried and tried, but nothing has happened." Her eyes raised and met mine. They were filled with unhappiness and need. "I want a child who can become a part of the new world we are heading for." I now knew the reason for the longing in her eyes when we first met.

I gulped. "Those are just stories. They aren't true. Ceres couldn't wave a magic wand and make sure anyone became pregnant and neither can I."

"Yes, you can. I know you can. It's in the record, Ceres is the goddess of fertility and you are descended from her, so you have her powers. You can do it." She reached over and put a hand on my lap. "Please. I'm begging you." Tears welled.

Ceres got that reputation because she knew plants. She knew which ones could help infertile women. But the unhappy woman before me would never believe it was that simple. Nothing would convince her that I couldn't help.

I made a decision. I would go for it. I would do what Ceres had done. I would use my knowledge of herbs to help this woman. I knew how because I'd heard the stories growing up. Knew which herbs increased a woman's chance of conceiving, had heard the recipe discussed. Knew how to mix them to maximum potency. "I might be able to get some herbs that will help but there's no guarantee."

Her smile turned the night into day. "I knew you'd do it! I knew I could count on your help!" She rose, filled with eagerness and the sudden energy of someone whose life has turned around. "Thank you, thank you, thank you!"

"Don't thank me yet. I need some specific herbs and I don't know where to find them on the Destiny."

"The greenhouses?" She leaned close, begging me to guarantee her a child. "They grow everything there."

"Maybe, but I don't work there. I can't just walk in and demand what I need. Unless you want me to explain what they are for." Which I was sure she didn't. She'd arranged a private meeting with me, she didn't want what she considered her lack to become public.

"I'll talk to Brian." Was the captain putty in his wife's hands? I decided he probably was, at least when they were alone. "He'll get you a job there." She waved her hands through the air as if painting a picture by Cezanne. "Brian will get you into the greenhouses." She wrapped her arms around me. "It's where you should be anyway."

My throat closed, and I let her ramble on because, as zealous as Darleen Smithers was at that moment, there'd be no interrupting and no changing her mind. And as she finally let go of me, I resigned myself to working in the greenhouses, at least temporarily. I listened to her until, running out of words at last, she drifted off to find her husband and play the gracious hostess by his side.

When the band tuned up, they were surprisingly good. I wondered how that could be because I'd not heard anyone practicing until I realized that all apartments were sound-proof, a wise precaution on a ship no one could ever leave. Cullen, still scowling, steered me onto the dance floor and we proceeded to waltz, polka and do a few other dances I didn't recognize. Not that I truly recognized the waltzs or polkas either because Cullen's dancing had clearly been learned during a required officer training class instead of being an inborn ability. I felt sorry for his teacher and was grateful when the music ended. As we passed the band, it was all the guitarist could do to keep a straight face.

Later, in the apartment, I realized that the band had whetted my appetite for music but what I wanted to hear was pan pipes. "Cullen…"

"Yes?"

"Would you play your pipes?"

"I don't play them. I told you that. I just liked the look of them so when I won them in a game of craps, I kept them." His look forbade arguing so I drifted towards my bedroom. Then he threw me a bone because we both knew he was lying about not playing the pipes. "You looked nice tonight. That green thing is pretty."

"The kitchen curtains?"

"They look better on you than on a window."

A compliment from Cullen Vail? I was momentarily stopped in my tracks. Then I continued on because the night was done, and it was time to go to bed. "I'm going to work in the greenhouses."

"Darleen Smithers? That was what she wanted to talk about? The greenhouses?"

"Yep."

"Why should she care where you work?"

I thought fast. "She knows I'm a botanist." I stepped through the doorway before he could say more.

But before I closed the door, he said, "You'll have no bodyguard at the greenhouses or anywhere else after this."

"You spoke with the captain?"

"I did. He agrees with you. The crisis is past. I'll make sure you have your own bike for transportation."

"And you'll have your own home again."

"Thank goodness." His tone of voice was unreadable so I couldn't gauge his relief at being free of me at last.

The next morning, he had breakfast ready as usual. Jelly donuts for me, a huge meal for him. His future children would start their day right while mine would barely survive.

I started my morning circuit of the room, nibbling as I walked. He said, "The captain called."

"Oh?" I licked jelly from a donut before it dripped on the floor.

Ramrod straight at the table he shoveled eggs into his mouth. "He's been busy. He must want you settled because you start work today. This morning." Juice went down quickly.

I had a job. A real job and had better get to it. "I'll take you to work today because you have no transportation yet but that bike I promised will be waiting when you get off work and keyed to your comunit." Almost like home. A surge of homesickness swept through me but was quickly gone.

I stuffed the last of the donut in my mouth and swallowed. Time to get busy.

The greenhouse personnel were expecting me when Cullen and I walked through the door but the only person who acknowledged me was the head grower and his expression would have killed me if possible. I managed to smile while avoiding eye contact and looked around for some sign of acceptance among the handful of people standing and walking around while pretending not to notice what was happening.

One young guy about my age or a bit younger smiled until he realized he was the only one doing so. Then his lips turned down and he went back to his work, pruning bean vines, while keeping up with what was happening though quick, furtive glances.

"Now that you're here, what do you intend to do?" The head grower, I vaguely remembered his name as Constance Reiwer, spread his legs wide and put his hands on his hips. What had the captain told him? Did he think I was in charge? Surely not, but my being there set him off like fireworks. "Elle Omstead." The way he said my name made my heart sink.

There are lots of people who hate our family because we are successful. Because success has been good to us. And they resent us for doing easily what they struggle to do. Constance Reiwer had undoubtedly heard about us and hated me because of my last name. And always would.

My voice squeaked. I hate confrontation and I'd never had to deal with this situation before, I'd always worked for relatives. "I was told to report to you." I stretched to my full five two and pretended I didn't know that he hated me. "What do you want me to do?"

He puffed his cheeks and looked me up and down as thoughts chased one another across his face. I was the captain's pet and, since the captain would undoubtedly be briefed every so often on my progress, he'd better give me something to do that sounded useful. But it also had to keep me out of his way and useless.

His eyes gleamed as the solution came to him. "I hear you've been picking apples." In one sentence, he put me in my place as a farmer instead of a scientist and came up with a job for me that no one could argue was inappropriate. "Check out the fruit trees. See if they are ready to be transplanted."

Where apple trees grew, other trees would be nearby. I needed berries from the Chaste tree for Darlene and it only made sense that the Destiny greenhouses would contain at least one of every kind of tree with food or medicinal potential. Including chaste-berries. But I didn't remember trees during my previous visits. "I don't know exactly where the trees are."

"In the farthest building. We won't see much of you." Which was what he wanted. Did he know it was what I wanted too?

He turned to the young man who had briefly smiled at me. He must be the bottom of the pecking order, the least important person in the room. "Saul, show Ms. Olmstead to the nursery."

Saul put away his pruning shears and came close and indicated with his chin that I follow. I understood his silence. If he wanted to move up in the pecking order, he'd better not show me any friendship.

Once we were away from the other botanists, though, Saul changed. Relaxed. Became curious. "The head grower said your last name is Olmstead?" I nodded. "There are a lot of Olmsteads in the agricultural business." I nodded again. "Are you related?"

"I am."

"Oh." That one word said he understood why Constance Reiwer didn't like me. I came from an influential family in the greenhouse business. He'd probably worked his way up.

We continued in silence for a moment. Then, "Why'd you stow away? Why not just apply as a crew member? They'd have been happy to have an Olmstead on board."

We were already deep in the greenhouses with the light from the artificial sun pouring through the glass ceilings. At night, when that faux sun went dark, grow lights would switch on so the plants could grow continuously. I touched the gauzy, green filament of a climbing bean plant and felt its satisfaction. The plants on the Destiny were finally making the transition from earth to space, thanks in part to me. The colonists would thrive and be healthy. I would only be needed if something went wrong. That would happen eventually, it did on earth and it would in space. But the first, most difficult part, was done.

I caught up with Saul. "I tried. I wasn't chosen. My genetic makeup didn't qualify."

He sniffed. "As far as I'm concerned, all that genetic purity stuff is a bunch of crap."

"The selection committee didn't see it that way."

"I suspect the selection committee was composed of genetic purists. They are bigots, you know, and there are genetic bigots on the Destiny. A lot of them." He shivered delicately as I recalled the crowds that almost made us miss the Destiny's launch. The anger, the hatred. I shivered too. "They spend most of their leisure time telling each other how superior they are to the rest of mankind. They have actually created a political action committee to get genetic screening for every fetus written into our constitution so no one with impure genes will be born. Ever."

"You're kidding."

"And they want to be the ones who decide what genes are acceptable."

"That's scary."

He nodded vigorously. "They meet in the restaurant in my apartment building so I hear them talk."

"I wonder if the captain knows."

"They aren't doing anything illegal. It's just politics, or so they say." He pushed a door open and a forest of tiny trees spread out before us. The nursery. "But if I were you, I wouldn't tell anyone about your genetic makeup."

I like trees, always have had a thing for them. The

quiet majesty of these youngsters growing towards a life of providing food made me glad to be an Olmstead. Made me glad for my unusual genes. "Mum's the word."

We were in the bowels of the greenhouse complex, passing through one building with no growing plants in it but boxes and barrels of what looked like chemicals. "What's all that stuff?"

Saul pointed. "When everything started dying, no one knew what to do but we knew the life of every person on board was endangered if we couldn't come up with a way of keeping the plants alive. So we tried everything, including every chemical ever known to boost plant production."

"Some of those chemicals are lethal." Nitrogen. Anhydrous ammonia. And more.

"It was a crisis. It was our job to feed the people on the Destiny. We'd have done anything, used anything."

I considered the boxes and barrels. "What will they do with all this stuff now?"

"Connie put in a requisition for it to be picked up. It just hasn't happened yet." He grinned as he pushed open another door and we entered a desert dry room filled with cacti. "Some things never change. On earth or on the Destiny, nothing gets done in a hurry." We laughed and made our way carefully around a few prickly pear cacti to still another greenhouse filled with small trees. We'd arrived at my work station.

He showed me around a bit, pointing out things that didn't need pointing out, stretching out his time in this special place. Then, smiling again so I'd know that at least one person in the greenhouses was my friend, he left, and I went to find the Chasteberry tree that would...or would not... help Darlene Smithers become pregnant. It stood in a corner and, when I explained my project, it was more than happy to help.

Chapter Twelve

A bike was waiting as promised at the end of that first day and when I got back to my apartment Cullen's things were gone. I should have been ecstatic. I wasn't. I missed him, missed his scowling presence, his dark eyes, that hair that never was out of place even first thing in the morning, missed the bulk of him in the room next to mine all night long.

I missed the way his eyes smiled at small children playing while his mouth held a serious line, the way he touched the apple trees in the orchard, lightly, seeing them for the first time in his life as living, breathing individuals. The way he shielded me from imaginary assailants and would have given his life to save mine.

That last was huge. I'd never thought of myself as needing protection but, remembering Saul's comment about my impure genes, the memory of Cullen and his protective bulk grew larger and larger as time passed.

Three months to be exact. Three months of happiness when I was alone with the trees and misery when other botanists were present. Except when Saul Darling worked with me because then time passed pleasantly, but that wasn't often. He never asked to be assigned to me because he knew he'd be ostracized by his coworkers if he did. Since I wasn't alone often, I decided to ask the captain if I could go back to my orchard.

Except it wasn't the captain who sent me to work in the greenhouses, it was his wife. So I decided to talk to her. See if she would forgive me for not helping her become pregnant. Throw myself on her mercy, try to get her to understand that I couldn't work magic, and ask to be returned to my beloved orchard.

So, instead of heading home one day after work, I strolled into the enclave of large houses belonging to important people. The place where Cullen lived. I passed his place and walked determinedly towards the largest house in the area, the captain's home. Darlene Smithers was just coming out, dressed in sneakers and jogging shorts, with a scarf covering her luxuriant hair.

She saw me, waved, and came running. "Elle! So good to see you."

How to start the conversation? Try a nice, safe topic. "You look nice." She did, too, though she resembled a teenager rather than the captain's wife. But I'd already figured that status wasn't important to Darlene Smithers.

A wide smile split her face. "Yes, I do look great and it's all your fault."

"My fault?"

She whirled around a couple of time. "Don't you know? Can't you see?"

"See what?"

She laughed. "I know I don't show yet, but I thought you'd know."

"You're...?"

"Yep." She grabbed me and hugged me hard. "I'm pregnant. Almost three months."

"Oh my gosh!" It had worked. My family's recipe actually worked. I shouldn't have been surprised but I was.

"You are a miracle worker. I'm so glad you stowed aboard the Destiny because I'm pregnant and that never happened before even though we tried practically forever." She let go of me and pulled me along with her. She moved along the sidewalk like an acrobat, half dancing, half jogging. She was that excited. "And I've made sure my friends know about you. You are much too precious a resource to keep to myself."

"You told someone?" I was horrified.

"Just a few close friends."

I stopped, unable to walk further. Such well-meaning gossip had done in more than one of my ancestors. All kinds of labels had been thrust upon us. Witches. Warlocks. The devils' spawn. Whatever the label, the result had been disastrous.

Darlene paused in her gyrations long enough to put her hands on my shoulders and look me in the eye. "I know you think what you do should be kept secret. But Elle, this is a new world, a new frontier. Old superstitions don't apply." She lifted her arms and spread them wide. "Those strange genes of yours are superior to ours, not the other way around."

She waggled a finger in my face. "So no more being stuck in that apple forest for you. Judging from the reactions I got from my friends, I'm guessing you'll be very popular in the future. Very, very popular. Every woman who doesn't conceive ASAP will be coming to see you."

Thanks to Darlene's fast gait that I now recognized as the exercise every mother-to-be needs, we'd left her exclusive neighborhood and reached the commercial section of Center City. It wasn't busy, no place on the Destiny was ever crowded, but at that moment every street had at least a handful of people heading home for the day just as I'd be doing if I hadn't gone to see Darlene.

Darlene Smithers was the captain's wife and used to being the center of attention, so she easily ignored the stares that came our way from a woman a few yards along the sidewalk. I wished I could do the same because the looks didn't seem like casual curiosity. In fact, they felt like poison darts. And, as I tried to figure out what was happening, I realized the woman wasn't looking at Darlene. She was looking at me. Just me.

What happened next happened quickly. The woman pointed at me and spoke at the top of her voice. "That's her. The stowaway. Trash genes on the Destiny." Heads swiveled as others looked where she was pointing, as eyes opened wide and mouths dropped. The woman stepped closer and snarled. "Time to throw out the trash!"

The others on the streets hesitated, unsure what to do. Then they took sides. Some turned and hurried away so as not to be drawn into a confrontation not to their liking. Some paused and watched unemotionally.

Others, a small group of three or four, joined the speaker and advanced towards us.

"Trash!" I wished they recognized the captain's wife because they might hesitate being nasty in her presence, but in her present outfit she was just another young woman out for a run. "Take the trash out!" Darlene backed up a step in horror, uncertain what to do. "Keep the Destiny clean!" She reversed her steps and came close, determined to protect me.

Someone carrying a bag of fresh vegetables reached in and withdrew a tomato. Just as a tomato had smashed against our windshield on launch day, one now hit me on the cheek. Then a second, only it didn't hit me, it hit Darlene's stomach.

She doubled over, using her hands to protect her abdomen. I felt her fear for her unborn child. "Run, Darlene!"

"I can't leave you alone." She took another step closer in spite of the rapidly advancing people. "It's my fault."

"Go. Your baby..."

More tomatoes pelted us, followed by sticks plucked from nearby trees. One hit Darlene across the shoulders. She gave me a wild look. "I'll get help. I'll call Brian."

"Run!"

She ran. Taking one last look at my attackers, I sought to hide. The greenhouses were close so I headed for the back door as fast as I could move. It was locked, of course, but it opened as I passed my comunit across the lock. The door slammed behind me but I kept moving, my legs pumping, throwing out mental pleas for help to the surrounding trees as I ran.

As quickly as that I was surrounded by shrubbery and was soon lost in a forest of green. Plants can't move, of course, but their branches bend and sway. Safe at last, I slowed, then stopped and listened but heard no sound of pursuit. I leaned against a sturdy dwarf walnut tree and then slid to the ground, shaking.

"Elle? What's going on?" Saul picked his way through the greenery and squatted beside me. "I heard a commotion outside and saw you run inside." His eyes dilated as he took in my tomato-splattered face and the cuts on my arms where sticks had found their mark. "Was it those gene-purity idiots?"

I was too stunned to say anything for a long time. I'd heard the stories of family members in similar situations. I'd shuddered and vowed never to suffer the same fate. "They called me trash."

He leaned back and regarded me as he thought over what I'd said. "I just wish I could grow things like you can. If that's trash, I wish I was garbage."

"Are they gone?"

"I'll check." He did and came back soon. "The last one is leaving." Saul was young and trying to do the right thing. "Come to the main greenhouse. We'll protect you."

"There's no one there. Everyone has gone home for the day." I pushed tomato from my arm. "Besides, do you really think they'd protect me?"

He rubbed the back of his neck. "I'm here. I will." But we both knew no one else would help him. "I'll go ahead and see if it's safe."

By the time Saul reached the first greenhouse and let me know that there was no one waiting outside, I'd cleaned up and was no longer shaking. But I still made my way carefully, looking ahead before entering each greenhouse, until I was in the main room. Sure enough, the sidewalk outside was deserted.

"I can't believe what just happened. Did they really call you a witch?" But Saul checked every possible nearby place someone could hide before gesturing to me that it was safe to join him. Then he stood guard as I got on my bike and took off.

As I zipped along the narrow path to New Rochelle that was totally artificial but looked like a rural gravel road, I realized I'd not gotten around to asking Darlene to speak to her husband about letting me get back to the apple orchard. I resolved to do so as soon as I could be reasonably sure that it was safe to be on the streets of Center City.

Saul said nothing to the other greenhouse workers about the incident. No one sent odd looks my way though Constance Reiwer did intercept a look between Saul and myself and pursed his lips. I hoped Saul could come up with a good explanation for our silent communication. I didn't want him punished because of me. Though young, Saul was actually quite a talented grower. He had potential.

Days passed and nothing else happened. I relaxed. Perhaps what happened was an isolated incident. But one day I learned that things were much worse than I could possibly have thought. It was Saul who knew what was going on. He suggested I learn what I was up against. He invited me to visit him at his apartment when the gene purist group was having a meeting in the restaurant that his apartment overlooked. He told me to disguise myself.

"Is it so bad that I can't be safe at your place?"

"It is that bad, Elle. That's why I think you should know what you're up against."

I braided my hair tight down my back and dressed as if I was a jogger, with a hooded sweatshirt thrown in for good measure and a headband covering what little red hair showed. Satisfied with the result, I parked my bike a few blocks from Saul's apartment building and jogged the rest of the way, huffing and puffing as if I was at the end of a long run. No one gave me a second glance.

"They meet in the outdoor restaurant. There are so many of them now that they pretty much take it over. The manager thinks they are a bunch of harmless idiots." He ushered me into a small apartment that overlooked the restaurant tables. With a window open we could see and hear everything. He waved me over. "The meeting is starting."

There were a lot of high-fives and good-natured chest thumps and lots of drinks were served. It was all good fun until the leader spoke. "We have new information about Elle Olmstead." Boos rose from everywhere. "The trash." That was followed by laughter. "The stowaway." More laughter. "You know where trash goes." There was more but I was so in shock I didn't hear.

When the speaker finally sat down Saul quietly closed his window and came close, gathering me in a hug that was exactly what I needed. "I wish you didn't have to hear that, Elle, but you needed to know. They hate you and every time they meet it's worse. I'm afraid they are building up to something."

"What can they do?"

"I don't know but I'm afraid for you."

I rubbed my forehead. I was getting a headache. "They are right about one thing. I wouldn't have been allowed on the Destiny if I'd applied."

"You have more talent in your little finger than the rest of us put together."

"Not that talent matters to those people out there."

"Tell someone in authority what we heard. You need protection."

I'd had protection and hated it. Guarding me had been Cullen's job and we were both glad when it ended. "I'll think about it." I wouldn't. "Thanks for the heads up. Now that I know what's going on, I'll be careful."

"Tell someone soon."

"I can take care of myself, Saul." I looked down at the crowd around the tables and couldn't help shuddering. They were eating and drinking and visiting each other, but in time the meeting would disband ,and they'd leave. If I was around when that happened, someone might recognize me even disguised as I was. I was suddenly afraid and needed to be gone. "I should leave while I still can."

"Take care, Elle."

"See you tomorrow."

I sneaked out the back of the building and walked two blocks directly away from my bike before heading back to where it was parked. I was that scared. As I kicked the starter I was glad it was electric and silent so no one could hear. I drove straight home and locked my doors, the first time ever. Cullen had locked them nightly but once he was gone, I didn't bother. Why should I? I knew everyone in New Rochelle and had no enemies.

Until now.

The following week was quiet, and I went back to trying to figure out how to get out of work at the greenhouses and back to the orchard. Talking to Darlene Smithers hadn't worked and I didn't want to bother the captain directly. He was an okay man but he didn't truly want to have to acknowledge my gift. I potted new saplings and watered older ones and sent those that were ready to leave into the wider world of the Destiny and generally threw as much dirt around as possible to work the fear out of me. Until one day when Constance Reiwer sought me out. I pushed mud from my face and wondered what he could possibly want. He usually ignored me as eagerly as I ignored him.

"The captain wants to see you." He shoved a request at me. "Clean up and head for the bridge." He carefully didn't touch my dirty self.

I cleaned up as best I could and proceeded to the bridge. It was my first time there and as I pushed open the door I decided the whole place had been designed to intimidate visitors. The captain was in a chair that fit his exalted status and was surrounded by a number of people who ignored him as they went about their jobs, the purposes of which I couldn't imagine beyond that they kept the Destiny pointed straight and true towards the planet chosen for colonization. Our new home, those of us who lived long enough to reach it.

He leaned back on his elbows and inspected me. "You're causing trouble again, Elle." I gulped as he shifted in his seat. "Every captain knows he can't make a journey without incident. You seem to be mine. Repeatedly."

"Sorry, Sir."

"There are people who don't think you should be here."

My heart sank. "I know that, Sir."

"They are growing in number and are more insistent every day."

"I know that too, Sir."

"They want you thrown in jail. Or worse."

My head snapped up. I squeaked, "Sir?"

"I told them that won't happen."

"Thank you, Sir."

"They aren't happy." He stroked his chin. "They read a lot of laws. I reminded them that, on the Destiny, I am the law but they didn't take that information kindly. I believe that protection is once again appropriate."

"No, Sir. Please."

One eyebrow arched. "No?"

"I'm safe in New Rochelle."

"The greenhouses are in Center City."

"I'd be happy to return to the orchard."

He stroked his chin and squinted in thought. Finally, he said, "Okay," and just like that, I was released from work in the greenhouses. I could do what I wanted to do. "Finish the week in the greenhouses, then go back to your trees."

I opened my mouth to thank him when he leaned close and spoke low. "When you get there, *stay* there. Don't come to Center City. Don't do anything to remind them that you exist. Their speech had the timbre of mutiny in it and I don't want to have to deal with a mutiny."

Every head in the place snapped around at his words even though they were said quietly. After that no one even pretended to be working as they waited to see what would happen next but he waved me away. The meeting was over. As I left, I felt the stares of everyone on the Bridge.

When I returned to the greenhouses, Constance Reiwer clearly wanted me to tell him what the captain had wanted but I didn't give him the satisfaction. The next morning though, when he informed me that the captain no longer wanted me to work in the greenhouses he smiled broadly. Not only did he now think that he knew what the meeting had been about, he thought it was because of him. He was getting what he wanted. Me gone. I let him think so.

As the news spread that this would be my last week in the greenhouses, I realized that Saul was the only person who would be sorry to see me go.

Chapter Thirteen

That was Tuesday. Wednesday and Thursday were routine except for a bit of time spent filling out the paperwork to transfer out and for arranging to return the bike once I no longer needed it.

I was so eager to have all the last-minute details at work done that I actually arrived early Friday and had to wait until Constance Reiwer got there and unlocked the place. As the other employees sauntered in one by one, they said goodbye and pretended to mean it. Saul was truly sad.

Constance poked a finger at Saul. "Time to check the oak trees in the nearby parks. See how they are doing. It might take all day." He knew Saul and I were friends. True to his character, he planned to keep us apart as much as possible on this, my last day.

So we went our separate ways. Saul imperceptibly shook his head and rolled his eyes in a look that said he'd find a way to see me some time during the day so we could have a proper goodbye. Then he headed out the front door and I went to the nursery at the back of the greenhouse complex.

There was a lot to do. I found myself surprisingly busy. By midafternoon, I was sweating and tired but confident that the trees would be okay with Saul. Of course, I'd already told him that he could come to me for help any time and I intended to repeat those instructions when he came to say goodbye.

I was in the middle of saying goodbye to the trees when a slight sound caught my attention. Outside of the greenhouses but loud enough to break my focus. Saul?

I looked but saw no one so I went back to the trees. Five minutes later, another sound came and this time it was Saul using his comunit to open the back door. "Hey Elle."

I waved him over. Letting the door slam behind him, he came at a half-run. He wasn't smiling. I rubbed a sore spot on my lower back. "What's up, Saul?"

"They are here."

"Who?"

"Those people from the restaurant."

My breath stopped. Those were the people who hated me. "Here? To see me?"

"I don't know. I didn't listen, just came around the back way to tell you. Warn you."

I thought. There could be a rational explanation for their being here. "Then I'm glad it's close to quitting time." I tried to laugh but it didn't come out right. "And I'm glad that Constance Reiwer is such a dictator. He'd never let anyone in his greenhouses who doesn't belong."

Saul stepped nervously from one foot to the other. "They were angry, and they were drunk."

I didn't want to panic unnecessarily. "All the more

reason for Constance not to let them in."

"I don't like it, Elle. You should leave."

"I don't intend to stay late. Not one second more than necessary. But I can't leave early. It would look funny and Constance Reiwer would figure out some way to use that fact against me. You know he would."

"Yeah, I do know." He heaved a sigh, then brightened. "It's almost time to leave. It'll be okay." He hugged me tight. "But be careful, huh?" I promised, and he picked up a sapling to transplant. Even though that wasn't his job today he couldn't ignore plants that needed help. He'd make sure the trees were okay when I was gone. "I'll give our boss my report on the oaks. It'll drag it out as long as necessary. I'll be around."

The next two hours dragged. We both jumped at every sound. When the clock finally said it was time to quit, we cleaned up with a hose and what was left of a bar of soap. I pulled my hands through my hair and we both dried ourselves on our shorts. Then we headed for the main greenhouse where Saul would give his report. He'd lie and say he'd been gone all day checking out trees and I'd punch out for the last time.

We didn't make it. While still deep in the bowels of the greenhouse complex, where there was no easy entrance or exit, we heard a sound. People. Several of them. Except there was no reason for anyone to be there. We were the only ones working so far from the main room. We looked uneasily one way and another but saw no one.

Then the lights went out. There was minimal faux

sunlight streaming through the glass ceiling but that wasn't much. The greenhouses depended mostly on grow lights spaced throughout the various buildings so as to provide perfect conditions for plants with differing light requirements. So though the greenhouses did take in light from our fake sun it wasn't much. Without grow lights, nothing would live. With them out now and just the light from outside, the place resembled a garden at twilight.

We could see but not clearly so we both jumped when several figures loomed mere yards away. Men, one of them carrying a glowstick so we knew they were responsible for the lights having been turned off. Why else bring their own light?

One of them pointed. "There she is."

The man beside him, larger and moving with the kind of swagger that said he was the leader, faced me. The man from the restaurant. The leader of the group that wanted me dead. "Indeed, she is here, just as we thought." He took a couple of steps until feet separated us.

Saul moaned. This was my fight, not his. "Run, Saul. Get out of here." I then whispered into my comunit to call for help, but it was dead. The lights weren't the only thing that had been turned off. Communication was also gone.

"I can't leave you alone with these men. They are dangerous." Saul was so scared he could hardly get the words out but he stood steadfast beside me.

"Go, Saul, and don't stop until you are where your comunit works. Call Cullen."

"Cullen Vail?"

"Tell him what's happening." I made a shooing motion. "Go!"

He ran, skirting around the group of men but they didn't stop him. They wanted me. I faced the half dozen men, feeling very alone. I couldn't speak until I took a deep breath, then I asked, as calmly as possible, "Are you people lost? We don't usually have visitors at the greenhouse."

"We're not lost."

"It's late. Quitting time. Everyone will be gone soon."

They laughed. "Everyone else is already gone."

"Not yet." I didn't know the time without a working comunit but I'd given myself extra time in case there was more paperwork to complete before clocking out for the last time. "It's not quite quitting time." I pretended to think. "I'm quite sure that if you hurry back the way you came, you can catch the head grower before he leaves."

"Nope. Won't happen. He's gone. They're all gone." He didn't come closer but he thrust his head forward. I could see the lines in his face. "We suggested they leave and they agreed. In fact, we insisted and they didn't argue."

No help would come. I gulped, trying desperately to think what to say next, to stall them as I gauged the distance around them. They were facing me and close but it was a large room. If I could sidle towards the wall, moving in what I hoped would seem an aimless motion, I might be able to break into a run and get out of there before they realized what I was doing.

The plants would help. They would hide me.

No they wouldn't, they couldn't, because we were in the room packed with chemicals that had been intended to be used as fertilizer that Saul had pointed out to me on my first day of work. There were no plants in the room. None to help me disappear.

But I had to do something. I had to try. I kept talking, heard myself babbling without knowing what I was saying as I ever so slowly moved sidewise. If I could get close enough to the wall where all those boxes and bags of chemicals were piled, I might make it. From the corner of my eye, because I dared not look directly anywhere for fear of giving away my plan, I saw that there was an opening in those piles. A small path through which I could see the door. It would be a tight squeeze, but I'm small and it was my only chance.

The leader took a step towards me, his lip curling as he got close. "You are an abomination. Trash. A female who'll contaminate our blood lines." Another step. "If we let you." Soon he'd reach me. "We're here to see that doesn't happen."

I moved. Dodging sidewise I ducked to avoid the arm that reached for me and ran flat out for that small opening among all those bags and boxes of chemicals.

"Stop her!"

They were too late. I was in what turned out to be a crevice in the piles and, as I saw the door ahead, I bent low and speeded up.

"Don't let her get away!"

They came after me but they were larger than me,

they didn't fit easily into that crevice and had to push the bags and boxes aside.

"Get her! Someone do something!"

The man with the glowstick threw it at me. It arced high in the air. I was running full out and it fell behind me as I reached the door to the next greenhouse, one filled with plants. I sent ahead a plea for help and the plants heard. I pulled a reserve of energy from somewhere inside of me and burst through the door, slamming it shut as soon as I was through.

A huge sound erupted behind me. I was so intent on running that I didn't dare turn to see what had made it. But the sound of shattering glass and the heat that swept through the greenhouse I was in told me what had happened. The mixture of chemicals that make up a glowstick give off light ,but they also give off heat. When it was thrown into those tons of chemicals that were never turned into fertilizer, the whole pile exploded.

It was going up fast. That first explosion was followed by another and then another. And still I ran, not daring to turn and see what was happening. I didn't know what chemicals had been stored in that room, nor did I know how much was in those bags and boxes but I knew that fertilizer can and does use ingredients that are used to make bombs. Such a bomb was now going off.

The only reason I didn't die was that the whole thing didn't go off at once, but the series of explosions behind me meant that the group of men that had come for me was undoubtedly dead or dying and I would join them soon if I didn't get out of there fast.

The plants did what they could. As I ran, they gave their lives to save mine, bending and swaying over me, taking the heat and pressure of the explosions. I felt their agony and heard their silent screams. They had no chance of surviving, their roots were anchored deep in the artificial soil but, in dying, they kept me alive.

For a while. As the explosions died away, the fire began, and the entire greenhouse complex became a flaming torch so hot that even the carefully controlled humidity evaporated as the devastation moved from one house to the next, following me as I ran, catching up to me before I reached safety.

Smoke roiled around me and that was one thing the plants couldn't help with. I had to slow down and, as the fire came from behind, the smoke got worse and I knew I was lost. And that I'd die.

"Elle!" Cullen's voice cut through the smoke.

"I'm here!"

"I'm coming. Keep calling."

I shouted his name over and over as I stumbled through the dark of that smoke and flame filled place towards the sound of his voice. Then something loomed in front of me and morphed into the solid body of Cullen Vail. I fell into his arms.

"This way." He half dragged, half pulled me until, with renewed strength brought on by the knowledge that I might survive after all, I found myself able to run through the smoke without help though, as for that, he refused to let go of me.

We went back the way he'd come until he paused because he was uncertain where precisely we were in that maze of buildings. I finally got my wits about me and asked the plants for direction, something I'd not thought to do while running for my life. The plants spoke. I pointed the way. Cullen, not asking how I knew, took off in that direction.

After what seemed like hours and was probably minutes, the smoke cleared, and we could see the main greenhouse ahead. It was filling with firemen in their unearthly gear. As we stumbled into the main room they stopped us and asked about anyone else in the path of the fire.

"There were some men. They started the fire. I didn't see them come out." I shrugged helplessly. A head nodded grimly because we all knew no one in that inferno could still be alive. Then he passed us by on his way into the smoke, followed by the rest of his crew.

We went outside. I gulped clean air, gobs and gobs of it. Pure, fresh air made by the plants that made up the farm that was the spaceship Destiny as I explained to Cullen what had just happened and who the men were who'd set the greenhouses on fire.

"I'm putting you in protective custody."

I'd been in jail for too many months. I planted my feet. "I'm going home."

"You live in an apartment. Difficult to protect. There may be more idiots out there."

"They don't know where I live." I hoped they didn't know. I threw Cullen's hand away from my waist and started for my bike. "And nothing you can do will stop me."

With a disgusted grunt that said something about not having the time to argue, he followed. Our bikes were nearby. We started for New Rochelle without a word, Cullen following closely, turning every so often to see if we were being followed, eyes roving constantly over the landscape. I felt totally safe though I'd never tell him that the fact of his being, of his character, of his commitment to his job and to me, contributed to that feeling.

We passed several vehicles on the way. They were filled with men and women pulling on fire gear as they moved and were going as fast as possible towards Center City. Communication on the Destiny was excellent. Hoards of people were headed towards the greenhouses to help fight the fire. The Destiny was a huge farming community but it was also a ship and fire on a ship is exceedingly dangerous.

With every adult in New Rochelle headed to the greenhouses, it was a silent homecoming. Only Wilkes Zander to greet us. His demeanor was somber. He noted our blackened appearance and put two and two together. "Are you guys all right?" Cullen nodded grimly and told Wilkes what had happened. Wilkes' eyes narrowed. "Think there are more of them?" Cullen shrugged, and Wilkes continued. "All of our able-bodied people are at the fire." His lips pursed. "But there are a few of us left here. Us old people, some kids and those adults not on fire duty. We're not helpless. We'll take care of Elle if anyone tries anything."

"I'll take care of her myself because I'm staying." Cullen pulled me around until I found my back against his chest with all of me folded in his arms. "Protecting Elle is my number one priority right now."

Wilkes nodded. "I'll keep watch anyway." He stood a little straighter. He was the mayor of New Rochelle and would protect its residents.

Cullen shrugged, and we went into my apartment where we took turns showering. It took forever to get the smell of fire and smoke out of our hair and off of our skin. When we were done we threw our clothes into a recycling bin. Then we pulled them back out and dumped them into the trash. No recycling for them, they smelled too awful.

Then we simply sat.

Time passed, I don't know how much.

Thoughts crept into my mind. Memories. Family stories about those of us who'd been thought to be witches. What had happened to them. Told quietly so we kids wouldn't hear, but we did and sometimes we didn't sleep after hearing those stories. Now they came back and crowded my thoughts. I sat on my couch in my apartment on the Destiny but everything faded and disappeared until all that was left was the horror of what might have happened because it had happened to some of my relatives.

I grew cold and wrapped my arms around my middle but it didn't help. I found myself shivering and couldn't stop.

The next thing I knew Cullen's arms were around

me and I was once again wrapped in his warmth and he didn't let me pull away. Not that I tried, I needed him but it didn't help. I couldn't stop shivering, couldn't get the pictures of those relatives out of my mind. Couldn't stop thinking of how close I'd come to suffering the same fate.

Cullen made a sound deep in his throat and left. I stood without moving, without knowing where I was or what I was doing, just that it was cold without him and scary. I looked to see where he was, to find him and safety once again. I saw him reaching into a pocket and bringing something out. The pan pipes.

Did he have them with him always? Did he play them whenever he was alone and had time on his hands? I'd thought the serenades in the orchard were special but perhaps making beautiful music was a part of his day whenever he thought he'd not be overheard.

Now he pulled me down on the couch and sat alongside me without our bodies touching. I wanted him to touch me, to warm me, to make me feel safe. Instead, he started to play.

His first song was Greensleeves. The music took me back to that night in the village square where I'd worn a billowy, green dress and we'd danced, though awkwardly, to music by the townspeople of New Rochelle. Was that why he chose Greensleeves? Our eyes met briefly and something flared. Then we each looked away.

He didn't stop with Greensleeves. He played for what seemed like a long time and was long enough for my shivering to slow and eventually stop. The music, some happy some simply beautiful, sent all those bad memories to the place of their origin, in the back of my mind where they belonged, along with other nightmares of childhood.

I reached out and lay my hand on his arm. When he finished the song he was playing, he put down the pipes and simply touched me. I smiled weakly. "Thanks. I'm okay now."

"I lied when I said I couldn't play the pipes."

"I knew you lied."

"And I knew that you knew."

We could have laughed at our little joke. Instead, we just sat some more, and I marveled that I'd got through the past few hours intact and with a warm feeling in the pit of my stomach instead of the terror and hatred that could have been there. Cullen had done that for me. To me.

Then he sat up straight and stiffened. Looked about, then settled back down so I wouldn't ask what he was doing. But it was too late, I'd seen his expression. "What's wrong?"

He rubbed the back of his neck. "I thought I heard something. It's probably nothing. A kid, maybe, playing ball, and I over reacted."

But it wasn't a kid. Cullen was experienced, he knew the sound a kid would make, and this wasn't it. I watched him intently. Watched his eyes shift from one window to another, watched his attention hone to a tight pitch. "What's wrong, Cullen, and don't lie to me."

He rose softly, stealthily. "Maybe nothing.

Hopefully nothing. But I'll check just to be sure." He moved like a panther to the windows and peered outside. Seeing nothing unusual he padded to the door where he stood listening for any sound on the other side. For a while he just stood like a statue, then he came towards me with one finger on his lips for me to keep quiet. He pulled me up and to the nearest window, still making sure we both made no sound.

Then he ever so slowly opened the window and gestured for me to climb out. There were no screens, none are needed where there are no insects and I was on the first floor. It was easy enough to slip through. Cullen folded himself after me and quietly closed the window. Then he pulled me towards a corner of the building, where he stopped and whispered, "I'm going to look. You stay here." And, like a shadow, he eased his large body close enough to the corner that he could see the entrance to the apartment building. A mini-second, no more, and he was back and squeezing my hand, still whispering. "Trouble."

"They couldn't have survived the fire." But there had only been a half-dozen men in the greenhouse. There had been a couple dozen people at the restaurant outside of Saul's apartment. "Many people hate me."

Cullen looked about. The field beyond my window was large and open and there were no other buildings close enough for us to slip behind unnoticed. We moved along the wall but no cover presented itself.

Then we heard voices, Wilkes Zander's in particular, asking with false conviviality what someone was doing in New Rochelle. He played the part of a nosy mayor to perfection, loud voice and all. To make sure we heard and knew danger was near. "To what do we owe this visit? New Rochelle is a lovely town but we don't get many visitors."

Evidently no one had expected to be stopped. There was a pause before someone answered. "We're looking for someone. She lives somewhere around here."

"And who would that be?" His voice louder still, he was warning us as best he could. "I'm the mayor and I know everyone."

Cullen peered carefully around the corner again, watching for a moment before coming back to me. His voice was barely discernable. "Wilkes is pretending to rub his arm but he's actually using his comunit." His voce was puzzled. He couldn't figure out what Wilkes was doing.

Suddenly, so fast that I jumped, a face appeared around the corner Cullen had just vacated. "I found her!" He grinned as his words filled the air.

In seconds they were there but Wilkes was there too, screaming into his comunit. "Emergency! Emergency! The baseball field!" Over and over until one of the men in the small mob struck him on the side of his head. He toppled over and didn't move.

"Elle, run!" Cullen grabbed me but this time it wasn't necessary. I was all primed to move so before the words were out I was skimming over the field, heading straight to the place I knew best, the place where I'd lived when I first boarded the Destiny, the one place where I might be safe if there was any safety on this space ship. The orchard.

Cullen was right behind me, pushing me when I slowed, turning and firing his taser as he ran. From a corner of my eye I saw two of our pursuers stumble and fall but the rest came on and there were way too many for him to taze them all. "The bikes," he yelled in my ear as we ran. "Make for the bikes. We can get away."

I shook my head, hair flying in a wind of our own making. "The orchard. I'll be safe there."

"Trees can't save you. I can."

But still I ran and there was nothing he could do except follow. As I ran I thought that he might be right, there's little that apple trees and cherry bushes can do. Maybe nothing. But I needed to be in that orchard, surrounded by things I loved. Needed to be there. Had to be there, no matter the consequences. Needed to at least feel safe.

Before we reached the trees, we heard another sound. People yelling, feet running. A lot of people. I took a chance and glanced over my shoulder. It seemed that every adult left in New Rochelle was congregating on the baseball field. They were confused at first, not knowing why they'd been summoned. Then someone pointed to Wilkes Zander lying motionless on the ground surrounded by strangers. A howl went up. And they acted.

We didn't stop running. We reached the orchard and kept going, slowing down only slightly until we were surrounded by greenery. We could hear the sounds of a melee in the baseball field but Cullen wouldn't let me stop to see what was happening. "Keep gong, Elle. You must be safe. You are more important than anyone back there. You alone can save the Destiny. You."

"They could be hurt." My friends, people I hadn't known until boarding the Destiny but who were now part of my life were back there. "They don't know what's going on."

"They'll figure it out." He steered me deeper into the orchard. "We need to find a place where the bushes are thick. We'll hide until that mob is taken care of by the good people of New Rochelle."

I was already headed for such a place. The place where I'd lived when I first boarded the Destiny. Where Alicia gave me Braveheart. Where the bushes and trees deliberately grew into a wall thick enough to hide anyone. I kept running and the trees and bushes parted as we went until we were sitting on faux dirt and leaning against a couple of dwarf apple trees.

I breathed, wondering if I'd breathed lately or not. I thought not. Cullen inspected our hideout. "It's thick here. It might do."

Of course, it was thick. I waved an arm. As we watched, the greenery grew thicker and still thicker until it became an impenetrable wall. Cullen whistled softly. "You did that, didn't you?"

"Not me. The plants did it."

"But you told them to."

"I asked, and they agreed." He whistled again, and I shushed him. "Now we should be quiet."

He scooted to where I was. In a gesture that seemed unconscious and probably was, he wrapped one arm around me and pulled me close. Then he whispered, "That's a handy gift you have. It's going to save us."

I peered into those stormy eyes. "It was my so-called 'gift' that almost killed us."

"I'd choose having the gift over not having it." One hand moved over my hair, getting tangled in all those curls until he had to pull it free. "You're one very special woman, Elle, and I'm glad I know you."

I had to press my face in his shirt in order to not laugh out loud. I wasn't sure it would have been hysterical laughter or not. It didn't matter, I could laugh again. "That's not what you said a while back."

"I know but that was then. This is now." With a small, satisfied sound deep in his throat, he slid down to a more comfortable place and leaned back. "So we wait."

"What do you suppose is happening back there?"

A lopsided grin lit up his face. "Knowing the good people of New Rochelle as I do, I suspect those thugs are wishing they'd never listened to all that ridiculous talk of superior and inferior genes." The grin grew, and he twirled a finger in the air. "In fact, I'm willing to bet that they wished they'd never applied for a spot on the Destiny." The finger made a slicing motion. "And when this is all done, and they face the consequences of their actions, I almost feel sorry for them. Almost. Because I happen to know that Captain Smithers doesn't suffer fools gladly. In fact, he doesn't suffer them at all."

I sucked in my breath. "The airlock?" Even after all they'd done, all they'd tried to do to me, I couldn't wish that on anyone. The specter of being shoved out the airlock myself was all too deeply ingrained in my mind. "I hope not."

"We'll see," was all Cullen would say as he pulled my head onto his shoulder and closed his eyes for much needed rest. "We'll see." And then, miracle of miracles considering the circumstances we were in, we slept. Cullen because he was used to situations like this and could sleep anywhere, any time. Me because his arm around me and his solid body against mine spoke of safety and a future that I'd not believed possible when I walked across that room so long ago and joined the colonists on their way to the space station.

Chapter Fourteen

We stayed in the orchard until we heard Wilkes Zander calling our names. Then I told the trees and bushes that we were safe, and they could let him through and they did. Wilkes' gaze went furtively from one side of the opening that appeared suddenly to the other, but seeing us he stepped through and soon stood before us, a blood-soaked rag around his forehead. "It's safe now. We took care of those guys. But you two need to come out so you can file charges." Curiosity was clear in his eyes but he asked no questions and we said nothing.

When we emerged from the orchard a small cheer went up from the group of New Rochelle residents armed with pitchforks, baseball bats and several tasers that had been taken from the mob of sullen men that they now surrounded.

Gerald came over and said what they were all thinking. "No one touches a hair on the head of any New Rochelle resident." An answering growl went up from the guards. "And you two are valued members of our community." I liked that they included Cullen as a resident of New Rochelle even though he'd only lived there for a short time. I gave Gerald a hug and gave everyone else high fives as he spoke to Cullen. "Security is on the way. They should be here in a few minutes."

By the time Security arrived, almost the entire community of New Rochelle was on the baseball field, watching the thugs and talking quietly among themselves as they tried to figure out what was going on but only Alicia spoke directly to me. "Braveheart is okay, Elle. I checked, and no one hurt him." She turned her face up to mine. "If anyone tried, I'd have stopped them. I'd have been real mean."

I thanked Alicia for making sure my kitten was safe, having no doubt she'd have done exactly what she threatened if Braveheart was in any danger at all. She'd make a fine mayor when her grandfather retired. I pitied anyone who tried to put anything over on her.

Then Security arrived, sirens wailing and lights flashing, and soon every single thug was gone as if they'd never existed. The faux dirt on the Destiny had the admirable quality of repairing itself. Every blade of grass was back in place and no scuff marks marred the perfection of the green landscape.

Cullen informed me that he'd been in contact with Captain Smithers and that we were to rest for the remainder of that day and report to him in the morning. He wanted to know who all had attacked me and what they'd done. In a grim voice, Cullen added, "They won't get off easy."

Cullen's bed was still in my apartment in the bedroom next to mine. When he'd moved out, for some unknown reason, I'd left the room intact. After a meal of canned soup because neither of us had the energy to cook or go to the café, he simply walked into his room and fell onto the bed fully clothed. I did the same in my own room but, unlike Cullen, I didn't sleep. Instead I thought.

Of everything that had happened since that day at the spaceport where my red hair had gotten me a place on the Destiny. Of the plants that had died and the other plants that were now thriving. Of the people those plants were keeping alive. Of the far-off planet that the Destiny would reach some day that would become a new home for everyone on the space ship I now called home. Of the fact that most of us wouldn't live to see that day. Of the Destiny itself, my home for the remainder of my life.

Good thing I liked the space ship those experts had spent so much time designing. Good thing they'd wisely considered that people who'd eventually become farmers on a far distant planet would make the transition more easily if they lived a rural life en route. And it truly was a rural environment. It was so much like Earth that if I stopped to think about my surroundings a lump would rise in my throat. Not from homesickness, rather because the Destiny was my home and I now loved every inch of the big, black behemoth.

The next morning, the captain was polite but definite. "Those men who came after you in the greenhouses didn't survive the fire, which is a good thing because it saves me the bother of punishing them." I didn't ask what their punishment would have been. I didn't want to know. "As for the rest of that group, they seem to be hangers-on. They're the kind of people who'll follow any idiot on a soapbox who convinces them that they are superior to everyone else."

"They aren't," Cullen said quietly.

"You're right about that and I'm making sure they get the message. I've declared martial law and it won't be lifted until everyone knows what happens to people who put the Destiny at risk." I gulped. "Their punishment will be severe."

The captain gazed into the distance at the still smoldering wreckage of the greenhouse complex. There wasn't a single useable building left. "They will rebuild the whole place, one stick at a time until it's back in business. And in their spare time, they'll work their asses off doing whatever chores Constance Reiwer can find for them so seeds of the kinds of plants they destroyed can be planted and grown. Then and only then will they be allowed to return to their lives and will martial law be lifted. No one will ever forget what happened."

"Seeds?" At sight of the smoldering greenhouses, my heart had sunk. No seeds from plants that had been burned to a crisp could possibly be viable.

A satisfied smile crossed the captain's face. "We have seeds. Billions of seeds, all kept in a safe. Fireproof. Explosion proof. Everything proof. Because seeds are our future." He leaned back and let his eyes rove over the ceiling and beyond, across that part of the Destiny visible from his command center on the bridge. Miles of greenery gently curving as it followed the inner side of the outer wall of the Destiny. "We did a good job when we designed this ship. The only thing we didn't take into account was the need for a goddess. Because we didn't know that we needed one." He pulled his eyes back and regarded me closely. "I know that now and am grateful that you stowed away."

A shiver crept along my spine. "About that goddess part..."

"Yes?"

"If it's all right with you, I'd just as soon no one knows that about me."

His brows knitted. "Why not? I'm in charge and I'll make sure no one harms you in any way at all. Not even verbally."

I took a deep breath. "I believe you. But this is a long-term thing. Future generations might look at things differently." I thought back to the stories I'd heard growing up. "People don't take kindly to anyone who can talk to plants."

His lips pursed. "They might see your descendants as witches?"

"It's happened before. It could happen again. If it's all the same to you, I'd prefer to remain anonymous."

He thought for a long time. "I'm not sure you're right about this. I think that in a new world, a new life, things could be different. But if it's what you want, then I'll agree. No word of your abilities will leak out." Humor gleamed in his face. "I'll even talk to my wife and make sure she, too, says nothing more of your...

um… abilities. And that she comes up with a story for those abilities of yours that she's told her friends about."

He rose and indicated that Cullen and I follow. "Speaking of Darlene, she asked me to bring you two home for lunch. If you have nothing pressing, I believe she's waiting for all of us." He touched my shoulder lightly. "Who knows, the two of you could become good friends. I know she'd like that and frankly, so would I."

We had a lovely meal and lingered over coffee afterwards. Darlene was eschewing liquor for the duration of her pregnancy and so didn't serve any but the coffee was delicious. She ground it herself, of course, from beans grown in a field just outside of Center City. Afterwards, the captain and Cullen had business to discuss so they disappeared into the captain's at-home office while Darlene led me to the garden behind her house.

It was lovely, with African violets rubbing shoulders with daisies, unlikely on Earth but not even worthy of mention here. I remembered the pictures on the walls of her home. She'd painted them herself. They were portraits of the flowers she grew. She had a green thumb and was a decent artist. I'd be glad to be her friend even though her taste in clothes tended towards kitchen curtains. Now she wore a pink flowing something draped over an ethereal body that already had a small bump in the abdomen.

"So what now?" She slid onto a soft chair and slipped out of her sandals.

"Now?" I sat primly on a nearby bench. "I guess I go back to raising apples and cherries."

"I mean what now for you personally. I'm not asking about your job, I know what astonishing thing you do for a living but that's not what I'm interested in at the moment."

"Uh." I would have scratched my head except it would have been childish. "What do you want to know?"

She laughed. Threw her head back and let it come from deep inside of her. It was a happy sound. Before her pregnancy such a sound would have been impossible. I was glad I'd helped bring out that happy laugh. "I mean what about you and Cullen. When are the two of you going to make it official?"

"Me and Cullen?" I asked stupidly.

"Who else? He's in love with you, you know, and you're in love with him though you hide it better."

"You can't know that about Cullen. No one can know what he's thinking. He's impossible to read."

She waved my words aside. "No, he's not. Remember that I'm married to the tough, military type. I can read my husband like a book and I can read Cullen too. He's in love with you and you're in love with him." She leaned close. "The question is what you are going to do about it."

"I... uh... haven't thought."

"Don't lie. You've thought about it."

"I haven't..."

She shook a finger at me. "Don't pretend you haven't given any thought to the future. If you don't have children, the future of every colonist on the Destiny will be in jeopardy. You must have children or the gift you have brought to the Destiny will be lost and people will die."

I sighed. "I know. And maybe I have thought about that. A bit."

"I suggest that you do more than think. I suggest you get moving and do something and soon before your biological clock starts causing problems for the entire Destiny." Before I could open my mouth to comment, she added, "From the way you've been looking at Cullen Vail and the way he's been looking at you, the solution is simple. But the military type doesn't talk about love easily. In fact, they seldom talk about it at all." She leaned close. "You must talk to him."

I shrank inside of myself. "I'd prefer not to."

She sniffed. "If you want to save future generations and you want Cullen Vail to be involved, you'll have to get the ball rolling yourself. Because he's the military type." She grinned slyly. "I did it and look how well that turned out. You can too."

At the sound of people coming into the garden, she put a finger to her lips. "They are coming back. Don't let them know what I said. But talk to Cullen. Tell him he belongs to you or tell him where to go so you can find someone else to father your children. But whatever you do, do it soon."

Chapter Fifteen

I spent the next week mulling over her words. She was right, of course and she was also right that the sooner I had children the sooner the Destiny's descendants would be assured of good harvests. Whether anyone else knew it or not was irrelevant. No one on Earth knew what my family did but we did it anyway. Now, on the Destiny, the future of ten thousand people and their descendants was at stake. That was huge. Darlene was right, I had to act.

So not long after my conversation with Darlene, when I was in the orchard checking on the cherry bushes while the apple trees deposited apples in my cart, I heard a sound. I turned and saw Cullen leaning against a tree and watching. "To what do I owe this visit?" Did he know I'd been thinking of him? Could he read minds? Was that why he was here?

"Just stopping by to check on you." He cleared his throat. "Make sure you're okay."

"I'm fine." I, too, was having trouble speaking.

"Actually, I came to tell you the news." He moved restlessly from one foot to the other. A sure giveaway that he, too, was uncomfortable.

That knowledge helped. Some of my nerves

dissipated. "Come, sit with me." I slid to the ground and patted a place beside me. He coughed a couple of times and joined me, carefully keeping his distance as I checked him from head to toe. "You said you have news."

"Yes..."

I wasn't going to say anything about him fathering my children. Not yet, not until I'd figured out how to approach the subject and at that moment I had no clue what to say. How to tell him.

But as suddenly as we'd sat on the ground, as quickly as my breath goes in and out, I knew that Darlene was right and that it was time and that this was the perfect opportunity to get things straight. To get on with my life, with or without him, no matter whether I knew how to phrase the thought or not. "Not yet Cullen. Before you give me your news, I have something to say to you. And it's important."

He looked at me warily, as a mouse might regard a fox before being eaten. "What?"

At that expression, all my bravery went out of me like a deflating balloon. I couldn't mention marriage or children. Couldn't. Didn't know how. But I had to say something, so I bluffed. "I want to apologize. I'm sorry for all the trouble I've caused." Just get through this meeting without making a fool of myself and start looking for someone else to father my very essential progeny. "I know that I've been a thorn in your side ever since we met."

"You were never that." He scowled. "Okay, maybe you were. No maybe about it, you were a huge thorn, a big problem. But that's all done and over with and I'm glad you are here because without you, everyone on the Destiny would be dead or dying."

"Thank you for sticking with me in spite of your feelings."

"Because of you the future is good. My future is good." He cleared his throat. "Which is kind of what I came to talk about."

I slid more until I was lying on the faux grass. I regarded the phony sunlight filtering through a canopy of thick, green leaves. No difference at all between Earth and the Destiny, never mind that the Destiny was deliberately designed. I reached as high as possible and brushed the leaves on a nearby cherry bush until they danced. The movement made me smile even as my insides churned because Cullen was beside me.

Something about the movement of those leaves and the possibility that they could be the last generation of leaves if I had no children changed my mind still again. Now was the time after all.

I didn't want to talk to Cullen about the future but I had to. Might as well do so now because delaying things wouldn't change anything. I'd gather my courage and ask him to father my children as soon as he said what he came to say. I decided I'd give myself that brief respite before making a fool of myself. "So talk, Cullen. What's your news?"

He didn't lie down beside me as I hoped. Instead he let his gaze wander along my body until our looks met. Then he sighed and spoke simply. "I spent the last hour with the captain. He was checking statistics for our new home. The planet we are headed for. He does that every so often as we get closer and closer because the readings are more accurate each time. The news I have is that our new home looks good. Very, very good. Excellent."

"That world is years away. We might not live to see it."

"Our children will."

"I don't have any children."

"Neither do I." He slid down then, at last, and moved close.

We stared upwards in companionable silence for a while. Then I spoke because the future lay ahead and couldn't be avoided. "I might not see that new world but if I have children, they will see it. In fact, they must because my descendants will assure that planet is fertile. They'll keep the plants alive that will keep the colony alive until it encompasses an entire planet that I might never know but that they will know intimately because it'll be their home."

"If you have children."

"No 'if' about it." I turned on my side to see him better. "I'd better have descendants or this whole trip through space will be for naught. That future colony will die if I don't have children."

"I've thought of that. You aren't immortal. Or are you? I never thought to ask."

My laugh was unexpected, even to me, and ended in a giggle, which made what I had to say easier. "I'm not. So I must think about the future. My future. My children."

"You must marry and have children. Or just have children, forget the husband. Husbands aren't essential to procreation."

"I'd prefer that my children know their father."

"Do you have someone in mind?" The words were spoken slowly. I couldn't read anything in his tone.

"Yep. I do."

"You do?" He drew his breath in sharply. He could hardly speak.

"I do. Because it's important."

"Congratulations." He sounded like he was about to expire from strangulation.

"Don't congratulate me yet. It's not definite."

"Why not?" He turned angry. "Any man will be lucky to have you."

"I'm glad you feel that way." The leaves turned greener as we watched. Lush and happy. Cullen looked at me suspiciously but I hadn't done anything.

"I haven't told him yet." The trees knew what I was feeling. Hope.

"Well then, tell me who he is and I'll make sure he understands what he's getting."

"He already knows me, both the good and the bad."

"There is no bad. Some thorns, maybe, but no bad. Whoever he is he should be jumping with eagerness to marry you. If he isn't he's an idiot."

"He's not an idiot."

"Then he'll be happy to marry you." A pause, then, "Who is he?"

"He's the military type."

"So he'll be a good father figure."

"I believe so. But he has a softer side, too."

"That's good."

"He likes music. He's a wonderful musician."

"I don't believe I know him."

"Yes, you do." Get on with it, Elle. Say it. "You know him well. Because he's you. Cullen Vail." The silence that followed lasted so long that I wondered if the trees would grow old and wither before we continued.

"Me?" Cullen's voice was an octave higher than usual.

What if Darlene was wrong? What if he didn't care for me? I didn't know what to say in the face of a silence that threatened to drag on so I babbled. "Of course, it doesn't have to be marriage. Like you said, lots of single women have children."

"Any child of mine will be legitimate. My parents didn't bother getting married and I spent my childhood shuttling between planets. My dad was on Mars and my mother on Earth and I spent a lot of time on space ships going from one to the other." He made a slicing motion as I realized what was behind his dislike of small spaces. Even the most spacious suites on shuttles are cramped and he'd said nothing about his parents being prosperous. "That won't happen to any child of mine. They will have two parents who are married to each other."

I thought that over. "Does that mean I'd better forget about you and start looking farther afield? Because you don't want to marry this particular thorn in your side?" I didn't look at him. The trees were lovely, I followed the intricate way their branches wove patterns against the pretend sky.

"It just so happens that I like thorns."

"So?"

"It's marriage or we go our separate ways." He was almost belligerent. "After we marry we can work on those children. Not before." He sounded like someone was strangling him but now the sound didn't bother me. In fact, it was wonderful. Musical. It was the sound of my future.

But he wasn't finished. "If you're not willing to marry me … and when I say marriage, I mean the forever kind … then start looking because there won't be any children any other way."

I began to smile. Couldn't help it. I wasn't a prude like Cullen but marriage would be my first choice. "Was that a proposal?"

He licked his lips but managed to plow ahead. "Maybe." Silence. "Yes." More silence, then, "It was. A proposal, that is." He ran a hand through his hair until, realizing what he was doing, he stopped. "What's your answer? Marriage with me or shack up with someone else?"

"Yes."

"Yes what? Marriage or someone else?"

"Yes, I'll marry you and yes we'll have the loveliest family imaginable."

"Really?"

Why did he sound surprised? Didn't he know we'd been moving towards this moment ever since he cornered me on the elevator going up to the space station? Why was I surprised? Why hadn't I known it?

"You'll marry me, Elle?"

"I can't think of a better way to spend the rest of my life."

"Really?"

"Yes, really."

Silence again, until I couldn't stand it. I rolled over to see what he was doing since he wasn't talking and found myself looking into his eyes. What he was doing was smiling. And smiling. And smiling. I moved a bit more, just enough to kiss him.

He tasted like the first time only sweeter.

He pulled away fractionally. "Do you intend to always initiate things?"

"If I have to. But that kiss was mutual and don't try to pretend it wasn't."

He flushed. "Yes it was." That smile again, but smug this time and that was all right with me, as he moved close and showed me that Cullen Vail, head of Security, knew how to do more than arrest people. He could kiss.

"The captain can perform the ceremony."

"When?"

He pulled back a bit. "As soon as possible. Sooner. After all, we owe it to the Destiny."

And so we did.

THE END

Did you miss Spirit Legend?
Did you miss Wolf Legend?